the 310:
EVERYTHING
SHE WANTS
beth killian

POCKET BOOKS   MTV BOOKS

New York London Toronto Sydney

POCKET BOOKS, a division of Simon & Schuster, Inc.
1230 Avenue of the Americas, New York, NY 10020

ISBN-13: 978-1-4165-2168-6
ISBN-10:   1-4165-2168-2

This MTV Books/Pocket Books trade paperback edition August 2006

10 9 8 7 6 5 4 3 2 1

For information regarding special discounts for bulk purchases,
please contact Simon & Schuster Special Sales at 1-800-456-6798
or business@simonandschuster.com

the 310:
EVERYTHING
SHE WANTS

Also by Beth Killian

The 310: Life as a Poser

For Susan,
who wanted something
to read on the plane.

acknowledgments

Special thanks to Barbara Ankrum, David Ankrum, and Chandra Years for answering my many questions about life behind the scenes, and to Eric Henderson for introducing me to the way of the cleat chaser. I owe you guys a kir royale.

the 310:
EVERYTHING
SHE WANTS

1

"So what do you think?" I held up a frilly lace camisole for inspection. "The blue or the purple?"

"Neither." My roommate, Jacinda Crane-Laird, grabbed a skimpy lace bra off the shelf at Smoulder, an upscale lingerie shop on West Hollywood's Melrose Avenue. "You want black. Black bra, black garter belt, black seamed stockings, black stilettos."

"Settle down there, Lolita." Coelle Banerjee, gorgeous half-Indian/half-Italian/All-American teen soap star and roommate number two, shook her head at Jacinda. "She's an eighteen-year-old virgin, not a Pussycat Doll."

"My point exactly." Jacinda looked around for an appropriately seductive ensemble. "If you ever want to lose that shameful status, you'd better start thinking—and acting—like a woman of the world." She snatched up a shiny black leather thong and steered me toward the dressing room. "Try this on. Danny will love it."

I dug my heels into the carpet. "I am *not* wearing leather underwear."

"You are so boring and puritanical. You know what you need?"

"A new roommate who's not a total perv?"

"No. You need to get laid."

I raised my eyebrow at the leather thong. "Not in that, I don't."

"Fine. I give up. You want to waste your life in a constant state of quiet desperation, go ahead." She smiled down at the thong, eyes gleaming. "I'll be living it up in leather."

"Have fun," I called as she disappeared into the dressing rooms, all bleached blonde hair and boundless moxie.

"Don't listen to the Doheny Drive Dominatrix," Coelle advised. "Pick out something you're comfortable in. If you don't feel comfortable, you won't look sexy, no matter how much skin you show."

"That's the problem." I sighed. "I can't imagine wearing any of this stuff in front of Danny without feeling totally self-conscious."

"First-time brain freeze? It'll pass."

"Yeah, I guess." I perked up as I caught sight of a fur-trimmed black negligee, then dismissed it as too Hollywood. No way could a small-town girl from Massachusetts pull that off.

"So have you decided when you're going to do it?" Coelle looked serene and wise beyond her years, as usual. She'd grown up as a child actor (think *Barney*, Broadway, and Nickelodeon) before landing a role on a soap opera called *Twilight's Tempest*, and was a seasoned professional at the age of seventeen.

"I don't know." I flushed as I contemplated the prospect of sex with my brand-new boyfriend, the divinely droolworthy Danny Bristow. "He invited me to go with him to this winter dance at UCLA, but I've got some bad associations with that. Look what happened when I got carried away at homecoming. And anyway, I don't want my first time to be in a dorm room or in the backseat of Danny's rickety old car. That's so cliché. I want it to be romantic, you know?"

"You could always spend the night at a hotel," she suggested, running her fingers over a display of ribbon-trimmed red demibras. "Valentine's Day is coming up. You guys could get a room at Le Parc or Maison 140 or maybe drive out to the ocean—there are some really cute bed-and-breakfasts in Santa Monica." She paused. "Does he know it'll be your first time?"

"Of course not. I may be a socially stunted pariah, but he doesn't need to know that. I told you, I want it to be romantic."

"Whatever. Just don't get so romantic you forget the condom. You don't want to end up the STD poster child like Jacinda."

"I heard that!" Ms. Moxie huffed out of the dressing room, glaring at Coelle. "And I will have you know that socialites don't get STDs—they are merely 'indisposed' for a few days."

"Relax. Don't get your leather panties in a bunch." Coelle grinned.

Jacinda turned to me. "So? Did you make a decision yet or are you still trying to find something that'll make you look like Little Bo Peep gone wild?"

"Some guys go for bonnets and pantaloons," I assured her as I surveyed the huge array of sultry lingerie. "Maybe you're right—maybe I should just go for basic black."

"Of course you should. Would I lie to you?"

"Uh, *yes.* Remember the first week I was here? The sabotage? The treachery? You were evil incarnate."

"That was ages ago. Now I'm your guardian angel."

"Ha."

"Listen, babe. You need to stop dwelling on the past and look toward the future: sex, parties, multimillion-dollar movie deals." She selected a gold-embroidered black bra. "Here, try this. Classic. Understated. Like a little black dress for your boobs."

"What there are of them." I sighed down at my underachieving chest.

"That's why God invented padding and underwire." She shooed me off toward the fitting rooms. "Scoot. We don't have all day—I still want to hit Maxfield and Lisa Kline."

Ugh. For a petite old-money heiress with wrists the size of Cheerios, she certainly had a lot of shopping stamina.

"Sir, yes, sir." I saluted and headed off toward the dressing room, where I squeezed myself into the delicate black bra, assessed my bare torso in the mirror, and tried to imagine Danny's response to seeing me in something like this.

The black and gold complemented my olive skin and dark brown hair (well, the extensions that now constituted the majority of my dark brown hair—long story). But I felt like a fraud in this expensive silk confection; the rest of my body was lanky, twitchy, far more Fruit of the Loom than La Perla. What if Danny saw through the fancy lingerie to the shy ex-tomboy underneath? What if he thought I was trying too hard and it turned him off completely?

Psychic link in full effect: my cell rang, and Danny's name flashed up on caller ID. I managed to wedge the phone between my cheek and shoulder while struggling to unclasp the bra. "Hello?"

"Hey." His warm, deep voice sounded even sexier when I was half-naked. "What are you doing?"

I wriggled back into my own bra. "You really want to know?"

"Sure."

"Trying on lingerie."

"I'll be right over."

"Excellent. I've been trying to hold myself back, but you know I have a total weakness for tall, dark, left-handed pitchers." I glanced into the mirror to find myself grinning maniacally. Hormones or true love? Who could tell? "Would you prefer me in black or red?"

"Both. Neither. Whatever you want." Clearly, color choices were the last thing on his mind.

"No, really. Let's say I'm lounging on a bed, pouting all seductively and batting my eyelashes in obscenely expensive lingerie." I tried to sound breathy and woman-of-the-worldish. "Would you like me better in red lingerie or black?"

"Is *no* lingerie an option?"

"You are so annoying." I hung up, put my shirt on, and stepped back into the main display area to find both my roommates huddled in a corner, whispering. As I approached, I heard Jacinda say, "Well, keep it to yourself. If she finds out—"

"If who finds out what?" I asked.

Both of them jumped a foot. "Nothing," Coelle said quickly.

"Yeah, nothing." Jacinda didn't meet my eyes. "So are you all set?"

I put my hands on my hips and stared at them. "What's going on?"

Coelle cleared her throat. "Nothing?" This came out as more of a question than a statement.

"What she said." Jacinda threw her long blonde hair back over one shoulder. "Nothing."

I narrowed my eyes. "Don't lie to me."

"We're not!" Jacinda insisted.

"Please. I can tell when I'm being lied to. Between my mother, my aunt, and my grandparents, I've been honing my lie-detector skills for years. And you guys? Are lying."

Coelle clasped her hands behind her back. "I have no idea what you're talking about."

"You know, for an award-winning actress, you're not very convincing." I bit my lower lip as I wracked my brains. What could they possibly want to hide from me?

I shifted my gaze toward Jacinda. "Is this about another mystery boyfriend?"

"No!"

Hmm. I glanced down at the bra in my hand. "Is this about Danny?"

"Of course not. You're being ridiculous."

Only one other possibility came to mind. "Is this about my mom?"

Coelle's eyes got huge.

"Crap." My hands curled into tight fists. "What has she done now? Was she in that gossip column again?"

"No." Jacinda stepped in front of Coelle. "This isn't about your mom and trust me, you should stop asking questions now."

I studied their expressions of anxiety and dismay. "Is this about my *dad*?"

No answer.

"Well?" I pressed. "Is it?"

"Can't we just get back to talking about sex and leather?" Jacinda pleaded.

"No! You know something, don't you? About my dad?"

"I do not," Coelle swore. "All I know for sure is what you know for sure: his name."

"Then why were you whispering like you were plotting to hold up a liquor store?" I demanded.

"I . . ." She threw up her hands. "Listen. I don't know anything for sure. But I heard a few rumors."

"About Anatole Farnsworth?" The father I'd never met, the father I'd been afraid to investigate for fear he'd turn out to be as bad—or even worse—than my mother, who was an abject failure as a parent.

I braced both hands against a glass countertop. "Hit me. Tell me everything you heard. I can take it."

Coelle shook her head so fast her earrings jingled. "No. Eva, listen, sometimes secrets stay secret for a good reason, and I think your dad's identity was in that category."

"What the hell does that mean?"

"It means I'm sorry I ever helped you break into your aunt's study."

Jacinda winked. "Don't worry, I'm not."

I glared at both of them. "This is ridiculous. You realize that I can just type his name into any Internet search engine and get all the information I want."

"Yeah, but you haven't," Coelle said gently. "If you really wanted to know about him, you would have Googled by now."

She had me there. I'd typed "Anatole," even "Anatole Farnswor" into the search box on Google, but couldn't quite bring myself to hit the enter key.

"I wasn't ready before," I blustered. "But now I am. I have a right to know whatever you know."

Coelle shook her head again. "Uh-uh. You'll have to find out for yourself."

My knees started to tremble, like my blood sugar had suddenly plummeted. What could be so bad that she'd stonewall like this? "Coelle. Seriously. Tell me right now."

But she refused to say another word, no matter how I begged. Finally, I moved on to Jacinda. "She told you everything, didn't she? Spill."

"What?" Her green eyes went glassy and vacant. "I'm just a dumb blonde bimbo."

"Save it for *Entertainment Tonight,*" I snapped. "Tell me or I'm slipping henna in your conditioner."

She gasped, her hands flying up to her freshly touched-up platinum roots. "You wouldn't!"

I smirked. "Payback is a bitch, baby. Spill."

"After you threatened my precious follicles? I don't think so."

I rolled my eyes. "You are impossible."

"You're impossible. I'm eccentric."

"You're too young to be eccentric," I protested.

"When your family came over on the *Mayflower* and you have trust funds up the ying-yang, you can be eccentric any time you like."

I pretended to gag. "Snob."

"Virgin."

"Slut."

"Prude."

"Ladies." The willowy redhead behind the cash register interrupted our intellectual debate. "May I help you find something?"

"No." I slammed the gold-and-black ensemble onto a shelf and stormed out to the street to interrogate Coelle, who had escaped while Jacinda and I traded barbs.

She was window-shopping a few yards away, still fidgeting and looking guilty.

"Hey." I fell in beside her, pretending to admire a display of sleek chrome furniture and abstract metal sculpture.

"Hey." She glanced down at my empty hands. "You didn't buy anything?"

"No." I kept staring at the window. "Just tell me what you heard about my dad, okay? Don't try to shelter me and spare my precious little feelings. I spent my whole life being sheltered by my family, and I don't need the same crap from my friends."

She shifted her weight and played with the ends of her long, black hair.

"Tell me," I said softly. *"Please."*

"You won't like it," she finally said.

"Oh, come on. How bad could it be?" I forced a laugh.

She looked at the sidewalk and prodded an old cigarette butt with the toe of her high-heeled boot.

"Coelle. I know my father's not perfect. Whatever fantasy I had about having some ideal sitcom dad out there, I'm over it." *Almost.* "My mom would never hook up with an ideal sitcom dad. So just give me the bad news—is he a serial killer? A crazy bigamist cult leader? A burned-out junkie rock star?"

She kept scuffing the sidewalk. "No, nothing like that."

I exhaled in relief. "Then what could be so horrible that you have to hide it from me?"

"You don't understand, Eva."

"Then *make* me understand. The thought of meeting him is the only thing that kept me going through all those years without my mom. What'd he do that's making you look at me like that?"

"He died."

2

ANATOLE FARNSWORTH, 56, of Bel Air, died January 14, 1987. After many years as a studio executive (most notably, president of production for Gawain Studios), Mr. Farnsworth was named chairman of Compass Pictures in 1985. Compass Pictures enjoyed unprecedented success with Mr. Farnsworth at the helm, producing blockbusters such as *Shooting the Moon, Guilty Pleasures,* and *Standoff.* He is survived by his loving wife of thirty years, Daphne Farnsworth (neé Holloway) and their three sons. Memorial services will be held . . .

I stared at the page I'd printed off my computer, rereading the obituary I'd found online that afternoon. January 14, 1987. That meant he'd died when I was only sixteen days old. Eighteen years of hoping and speculating about what he might be like, and he'd been dead this whole time.

You'd think I'd have some strong emotional response to this—rage, grief, even relief—but I just felt numb. Absolutely empty. I fidgeted in the black leather chair in the Allora Agency waiting room and stared down Harper Hollings, the sadistic blonde assistant behind the glass-and-metal reception desk. "Are you going to tell Laurel I'm here or what?"

"Laurel's in a meeting," she replied, cool and condescending as ever.

"She's always in a meeting. What I have to say to her is a lot more important than whatever she's doing right now. Trust me."

"More important than solidifying a three-picture deal? I don't think so, princess."

She had despised me from the moment I'd set foot in Los Angeles International Airport last month. As the newest trainee for my aunt Laurel, who was the hottest agent in town for actors twenty-one and under, Harper resented every single second she had to spend being civil to me instead of stabbing her competition in the back with a Mont Blanc fountain pen.

I glanced at the huge clock over the reception desk. "I'm waiting five more minutes and then I'm going in with or without your permission."

She didn't deign to respond, just sniffed loudly and went back to answering phones.

I watched the minutes tick by, then made a big show of waving my sheet of paper as I got to my feet. "A pleasure as always, Harper."

She shot back in her wheeled ergonomic leather chair, "I *told* you, Laurel's *busy.*"

"She doesn't even know I'm here," I reminded her.

"Because she's *in a meeting.*" She marched around the desk and placed a restraining hand on my shoulder. Her French manicure was perfect, her Cartier watch obnoxiously shiny. "Sit down and wait your turn."

I wrenched away from her grip. "Unless you want that watch ticking in your esophagus, do not start with me today." Then I shoved past her and made a break for the closed door to Laurel's office.

"Come back here!" Harper charged after me but, as she was wearing impractical high-heeled pumps and I was in sneakers, I easily outpaced her.

"You had your chance!" I cried, racing past the white walls and abstract art prints toward the end of the hall.

Her fingertips brushed my shoulder but she was too slow—I yanked the door handle and burst into my aunt's office.

"Evie?" Laurel looked up from the contract she was reading. Her office was like a living advertisement for Armani— she looked effortlessly chic in one of her customary black tailored suits and the two hair-gelled, ubertanned men seated across the conference table oozed corporate authority in well-cut dark jackets and trousers.

"I tried . . . to stop her." Harper leaned heavily on the

door frame, holding her side with one hand and panting from the exertion of our fifty-yard dash. "I told her . . . you weren't to be disturbed, but she can never take no . . . for an answer . . ."

"That's because she takes after me." Laurel smiled wryly. "Eva, this is Seth Becker and Jason Hein. Gentlemen, this is Eva Cordes, my niece and latest client. She's already done a national commercial and she's gearing up to be the next big thing in Hollywood."

"Well, she already knows how to make a very dramatic entrance." Seth didn't bother trying to hide his irritation at being interrupted.

"Yes, she does." Laurel arched one immaculately plucked brown eyebrow. She was certainly in an indulgent mood—I'd expected her to, like, eviscerate me with a letter opener when I barged in on a meeting. But she kept smiling, all calm and relaxed. Weird. "What can I do for you, pet?"

I thrust the obituary at her. "You can tell me what happened to my father."

She covered her mouth as she scanned the text. Then she lifted her gaze to meet mine. "How did you find out about this?"

"I'm not as stupid as you and Mom think I am." I planted both hands on the table and leaned forward into her personal space. "I want some answers. Right now."

Seth and Jason were both shooting curious glances toward the paper, so Laurel clutched it against her chest and rose to her feet. "Gentlemen, I'm afraid we're going to have to reschedule."

Harper gasped. "You're going to let her get away with this?"

Laurel pinned her assistant with a Sub-Zero glare. "Harper, if you're not back in that front office in thirty seconds, you can find a new agency to overwork and underpay you."

Harper turned on her burgundy Ferragamo pumps and fled the room.

Seth and Jason gathered up the contracts spread over the table and bundled them into black leather briefcases. "Have your assistant call our assistants," Seth said. "We'll set up a meeting next week. Maybe lunch?"

Laurel shook her head. "I'm booked solid next week. It'll have to be breakfast."

Seth gave me the evil eye as he humbled himself to accept a lowly breakfast meeting. "I'll be in touch."

"Thanks. Sorry for the interruption, but . . ." she gestured to me as if to say, *Kids today! What are you gonna do?* "Bit of a family emergency."

"No problem whatsoever." Seth and Jason strode out the door, leaving only a cloud of disgruntlement and expensive cologne in their wake.

The instant the door closed behind them, Aunt Laurel clicked the lock shut and whirled around, her eyes brimming with panic. "Okay, Eva, you have to believe me: Anatole Farnsworth was not your father."

I boosted myself up to sit on the conference table. "Stop your lies. I know the truth."

She crossed her arms, trying to gauge how much I knew

and whether I was bluffing. "What makes you say that?"

I tossed my head. "I went through your study when I was taking care of your dog last month."

She gasped. "You *didn't.*"

"Oh yes. I read all the letters Mom wrote to you in the eighties. I know this guy's my dad."

She started rubbing her forehead. "You don't."

"I do." I set my jaw and waited for her to crack. "You can't fool me anymore. I know what happened."

She opened her mouth, then closed it, then opened it again. "Okay, first of all, just because you found some documents *suggesting* that Anatole Farnsworth is your father does not mean that you know everything. Trust me."

"I'm done trusting you. And the documents I read didn't *suggest* anything. The facts are right there in black and white. I read Mom's note from the hospital."

"I . . ." Her composure disintegrated again. "You were never supposed to find out about this."

"Why not?" I demanded. "He's dead; what difference does it make whether I know or not?"

She sagged back against the locked door.

"What? What is so scandalous that I never heard word one about this guy? Why did Mom never break down and spill her guts? That's the only secret she's ever kept for over a week."

"Evie, I know you feel betrayed, but you have to understand—"

I held up my hand. "If you say you were just doing this for my own good, I'm going to go nuclear. Seriously. Harper will have to call in the LAPD and we'll be the lead story on the evening news."

"Fine, then." She shrugged. "I won't say it."

"Good. I'm eighteen; I don't need anyone to shield me from the cold, cruel world. What I do need is for everyone to stop with the constant lying. So one more time: Is Anatole Farnsworth my father?"

A long, resigned sigh. "Yes." And then: "Your mother is going to kill me."

"No, she won't," I scoffed. "If she killed you, she couldn't stay in your guesthouse anymore. Although she would inherit all your clothes and jewelry—she'd like that."

"Try to show a little more respect for Marisela, pet," she said in a tone that suggested she didn't really mean it.

"Why? Because she tells her boyfriends I'm her younger sister instead of her daughter? Because she dumped me with my grandparents to raise when I was three years old? Because she did a ton of drugs and had me out of wedlock with some smarmy film executive who was cheating on his wife?"

"Your mother has had a very difficult life," Laurel said.

"Yeah. I'm sure being a supermodel was really hard. All the money, the first-class flights to Paris, the adoring fans . . . sounds excruciating."

"If you become famous, you'll understand. You think it's so easy and glamorous, but that lifestyle comes with a very high price tag."

"So why does she still act like a dramaholic eighth grader when she's not even famous anymore? And why did she sleep with married men? Doesn't she have any pride?" I paused. "Never mind; I already know the answer to that."

"You don't have to be best friends with her—"

"No kidding," I muttered.

"—but try to show some compassion."

"Screw that. You told me I shouldn't expect anything from her? Well, she shouldn't expect anything from me. She's *my* parent, not the other way around."

My aunt ran her hand through her dark brown hair. "You and your mother. This is why I have my little poodle baby instead of a husband and kids."

Ha. Her so-called baby was a vicious, bloodthirsty eight-pound attack dog named Rhett. Rhett could make mincemeat of a rottweiler any day, and he hated everyone except Laurel and Danny.

But I would not be distracted by dog talk. "Why didn't you guys tell me he was dead? You could have saved me years of pointless speculation."

"I know, but ultimately it was your mom's call. You'll have to talk to her about all of this."

"Well, can you at least tell me how he died? All the obituaries I found were really vague. 'Sudden illness' and all that."

She nodded. "He was on the tennis court one morning and he collapsed. A heart attack, I think. He wasn't that old—"

"Fifty-six," I supplied.

"But I guess all the smoking and the stress got to him and he just keeled over in the middle of a round of doubles."

"And he was a powerful guy in Hollywood?"

"Extremely powerful. He was a studio head."

"So what did he say when he found out about me? Did he get to see me before he died?"

"I don't know. I honestly don't. Ask your mother."

Easier said than done. "Is she back from Scottsdale yet?" My mother, in the throes of her last emotional breakdown (which, if you ask her, was caused by me, but if you ask me was caused by her own reckless disregard for the truth), had fled to Arizona for a few weeks of spa treatments funded, of course, by Laurel "the Enabler" Cordes.

"Is there any chance at all you'll believe me if I say no?"

"No."

"Then yes, she's back from Scottsdale and helping herself to all the amenities of my guesthouse."

"How nice of her to call me and let me know she's back in town," I said dryly. "I guess we're due for another one of our famous family dinners."

But my aunt shook her head. "Don't drag me into this again. This is between you and Marisela. I've already gotten way more involved than I meant to."

"So now you're just going to punk out and make me deal with her all by myself?"

Ding, ding, ding. I'll make sure she's in the guesthouse tomorrow, but that's as far as I go."

"But you know she's just going to be . . ." I tried to find words to accurately describe my mother " . . . the way she always is."

"It's between you and her," Laurel repeated. "But good news—I was going to surprise you with this later, but I might as well tell you now: I bought you a car. So you can get around town by yourself. Harper will deliver it to your apartment later this afternoon."

I blinked. "You did?"

"Mm-hmm. Who's the greatest aunt in the world?" She smiled, at which point I noticed the healthy pink flush in her cheeks and the sparkle in her eyes.

Hmm. Was this a trap of some sort? Would I pay for this later? "Why are you being so nice all of a sudden?"

"I'm always nice."

"Yeah, but a *car*?"

Her smile vanished as she drummed her fingers on the glossy mahogany desktop. "You know, gifts can always be returned if the recipient isn't suitably grateful."

"I'm grateful, I'm grateful," I assured her. "Now I won't have to depend on Bissy Billington and her mother for rides to acting class."

"They're still mad at you about the sunless tanner commercial?"

"Mrs. Billington is convinced her precious Bissy would've been the one shaking her booty on national TV if it weren't for my devious tricks."

"That woman always had more hair mousse than brains. Well, watch out for them. Hell hath no fury like a Texas beauty queen scorned." She opened the door and ushered me into the hallway. "And while we're on the subject, try to make a fresh start in acting class, okay? Smith is finally back on his feet."

Smith, our tattooed and tormented acting coach, had broken his tailbone a few weeks ago during an unfortunate accident involving an acting exercise that required us to get in touch with our inner wild beasts, a water bottle hurled across the room at top speed, and, well, me.

"That wasn't my fault," I insisted for the hundredth time.

"Just be on your best behavior, okay?"

"I will," I vowed. Little did she know I had no intention of ever going to Smith's class again. And that I was still seeing Danny after she had specifically declared him off-limits. She had her secrets, I had mine.

"I'll make sure your mom's ready to talk to you tomorrow," she promised, her unnerving, cheery smile returning. "And you'll get the car in a few hours. Do you need anything else?"

A nonmortifying, semifunctional family, for one. "Nope," I said breezily. "I'm good. And I can't wait to see my car!"

She lowered her voice as Harper flounced off toward the espresso maker in the next room. "Did you really break into the file cabinets in my study?"

"Hell yeah." I tried to sound rebellious.

She nodded, then stared down at her sensible black shoes for a moment before clearing her throat and asking, "So you know about the . . . that, uh . . ."

"That my mom got pregnant again after she had me?" I prompted. "Yeah. Read all about it."

"Shit."

"And all these years I thought I was an only child." I strode toward the massive glass doors. "Mom and I sure have lots to discuss, don't we?"

3

"Guess what? I have a new boyfriend," Coelle announced when I returned to the apartment. "It's fairly serious, but of course we're telling the press we're just friends."

I'd hoped to escape up to my bedroom to mull over the newest revelations about my father, but privacy was a rare commodity in the small, low-ceilinged West Hollywood hovel I shared with Jacinda and Coelle. Our apartment was two stories, and the only way to get upstairs was to pass through the living room and kitchen, both of which were so completely covered with Jacinda's designer castoffs ("Once I've been photographed in an outfit, I can't possibly wear it again!") that we couldn't actually see the carpet anymore.

"A new boyfriend?" I touched the folded obituary that I'd shoved into my jeans pocket and tried to find the quickest way through this conversation. "Weren't you single this morning?"

"Yep." Coelle grabbed the remote control from Jacinda (a hopeless E! junkie) and switched to Animal Planet. "But the *Twilight's Tempest* producers decided that a high-profile romance will boost ratings for the show, along with my Q rating. So as of three P.M. today, I'm dating Quentin Palmer."

"What's a Q rating?" I asked, trying to update my Hollywood lexicon.

"A quantified measure of the familiarity and appeal of a performer to the general public," Jacinda rattled off. She was decked out in her version of sloppy sweats—a button-down white Barbour shirt, a canary diamond pendant, and the patent leather thong she'd just purchased at Smoulder

"What'd you do, memorize the SAG handbook?"

"South of Sunset," she corrected. "They just ran a big article on how to compute Q ratings and who's rising and falling. I'm rising, of course."

"Of course." I couldn't look away from the dominatrix thong. "Do you mind covering up? Or at least changing into undies that keep your butt off the couch I have to sit on?"

"Hey, some of us are comfortable with our bodies, Snow White."

"But doesn't that, like, chafe?"

"You have to suffer to be beautiful." She kicked her feet up onto the coffee table and beamed.

I gave Coelle the look we always gave each other over Jacinda's exhibitionism. "Have you *ever* had any shame?"

"Shame is so bourgeois," she scoffed. "Besides, I have to break this in. Now that I'm single again, who knows who I might hook up with? I need to be ready at all times."

Realizing that I was completely outgunned in this battle of wills, I turned back to Coelle. "So Quentin Palmer, huh? How long has he been on the show?"

"Only a few months. He plays Bart Vanderputten, the black sheep of the Vanderputten family, and he's the love interest for my character. He's twenty-one, I think."

"You think? Shouldn't his girlfriend know how old he is?"

"It's only my first day on the job." She held up a folder stuffed with photos and press clippings. "His manager gave me a whole portfolio. I'm studying up so I'll be ready for the reporter questions at our first official red carpet appearance."

Jacinda peered over at the head shots of the square-jawed, dark-haired actor. "Ooh, he's hot."

"Yeah, where do they find these genetically flawless guys?" I cast an appraising glance at the photos—Quentin looked kind of like Jake Gyllenhaal. "I'd rather study that than those endless lists of vocab for the SAT."

"Well, as soon as I memorize his astrological sign, favorite food, and stance on the boxers-versus-briefs issue, I'll be right back to 'deleterious' and 'draconian.'" Coelle had decided that she needed to score in the top seventh percentile of the SAT to compensate for her unconventional education—a series of on-set tutors—and secure her entry to Cornell. She was obsessed with quitting acting and becoming a veterinarian, a career which would fulfill her desire to work with animals, with the added benefit of pissing off her mother.

Jacinda was still slavering over the picture of the new costar. "Is his name really Quentin Palmer? Because I don't know if I could date someone named Quentin."

"Luckily, you don't have to date him; I do." Coelle flipped through her new man prospectus. "And according to this, he was born David Gellar. But Sarah Michelle already has a lock on Gellar and I guess David was too boring for a soap opera cast member, so . . ."

"Doesn't anyone around here use their real name professionally?" I asked.

Jacinda raised one hand, using her other hand to snatch back the remote and switch the TV back to E!.

"Anyone who *didn't* go to prep school with a bunch of Rockefellers and Guggenheims?"

Jacinda put down her hand.

Coelle shrugged. "I use my real name. It's spelled wrong, of course, but . . ."

"What do you mean, it's spelled wrong?" I asked.

"Well, my name means 'nightingale' in Hindi. My dad chose it, and it's supposed to be spelled K-O-E-L. But my mom said that looked too masculine and no one would know how to pronounce it, so she had them spell it all Frenchy on the birth certificate."

Coelle's mom was the opposite of mine: all over her daughter like a starving cat on a can of Fancy Feast. According to Coelle, the only reason they were both still alive was that her father had forced her mother to stay in New

York City when Coelle moved out to California two years ago.

I returned my attention to the Gyllenhaal-esque costar. "So you've never been out with David-slash-Quentin before, but now you're his one true love?"

"Only in front of the cameras. Off-camera we don't even have to speak to each other. He's my POB: my photo-op boyfriend. And neither of us can date anyone else without it turning into a whole faux-cheating scandal, but luckily I don't have time to date anyone anyway."

"You need new representation, babe." Jacinda popped open a fresh can of sugar-free Red Bull. "A pretty little thing like you can do way better than a C-list soap guy. Want me to make a few phone calls for you?"

"The whole point is to generate publicity for our show," Coelle reminded her. *Twilight's Tempest* has a lot of die-hard fans, and they want to see couples on the show dating in real life."

"You're not gonna be on daytime TV forever and you have your own career to think about. Let me talk to my people—I could get you a real celeb. I could launch you into the stratosphere."

"I don't want to be launched into the stratosphere," Coelle countered. "I want to turn eighteen, quit the show, go to college like a normal kid, and tell my mom to get out of my life. Oh, and start therapy. I definitely need therapy."

"As long as you've got a plan," I said. "So is this how the real Hollywood insiders date? It's all arranged by managers and agents and producers? That's so . . ."

"Pathetic?" Jacinda wrinkled up her nose in disgust. "I know. I'd never let anyone tell me who I could and couldn't date. But then again, I wouldn't be caught dead giving my number to anyone less than a true superstar."

"Says the girl who has topless photos cluttering up every in-box spam filter from here to Singapore." Coelle snorted.

"Shut up! That was a momentary lapse in judgment!" Jacinda flushed.

"And the little trip we all just took to the free clinic in the Valley?"

"A simple misunderstanding. Could've happened to anyone," she blustered. "When you're as gorgeous and high-profile as I am, you're not allowed to make mistakes like the plebs. Gossip columns are so vicious."

I sat down between them before Jacinda could scratch Coelle's eyes out. "I'm starving. Who wants dinner?"

"I do, but only if we go somewhere I can get fries." Jacinda, though a wispy size two, had the appetite of a truck driver with a tapeworm. If it wasn't on a drive-thru menu, she wasn't interested.

"I do, but only if we go someplace healthy," Coelle said at the same time. "I'm only eating salad this week. Salad and water."

"Even for breakfast?" I pressed.

"Miss quote-unquote 'recovered' bulimic here doesn't do breakfast," Jacinda said disapprovingly.

"You're the one with the eating problem," Coelle shot back. "All that sugar and salt is going to totally ravage your hair and skin. At least salads have nutritional value."

"Hey, I had a Jamba Juice yesterday. I'm set for vitamin C for the rest of the week!"

I clamped my hands over my ears. "Forget it. If you guys are going to bicker all night, I'll eat by myself. I have a lot on my mind, anyway."

Coelle and Jacinda exchanged conspiratorial glances. "Did you ask Laurel about your dad?"

"Yeah."

"And?"

"And I'm not ready to talk about it yet." I headed toward the staircase. "But she bought me a car."

"Score." Jacinda turned back to the TV and readjusted the leather thong, which had to be giving her a monstrous wedgie. "What kind?"

"I don't know yet. But she was in a freakishly good mood, so I'm thinking something sleek, shiny, and cherry red."

"Wow." Danny Bristow pushed back the brim of his ever-present UCLA baseball cap and stared at the hulking vehicle Harper had dropped off for me. "That's quite a car."

"Go ahead and say it—I might as well be driving a tank."

He rocked back on his heels. "Finding street parking for that thing is gonna suck."

"I know!" My fantasies of Benzes and Bentleys and Beemers (oh my!) evaporated as I cringed at the boxy white van Laurel had given me. The vehicle was as huge as it was ancient, with rust creeping in at the wheel wells and three rows of seats inside. And a little net for groceries in the back. "How old does she think I am? Forty? And the mother of sextuplets?"

Danny squeezed my hand. "Well, at least you can fit all your friends in, plus a keg or three. You'll be the road trip queen of Southern California. And if you squint, it's kind of retro."

I shook my head. "No. Retro would be *your* car." I nodded toward his '84 gold Mercedes sedan, a precarious automotive balance of loving restoration and imminent collapse. "But this . . . this is the Moby Dick of cars."

He grinned. "I didn't even know they still made vans like this."

"They don't! According to Harper, this was a showroom demo that sat on the used car lot for years before Laurel finally got it for, like, free."

"How many years? Ten? Fifteen?"

"You're not helping!" I jabbed him with my elbow. "I know I should be weeping with gratitude just to have a car at all, but seriously, when Coelle and Jacinda see this—"

"Oh. My. God." Jacinda's voice piped up behind me. "What is that *thing*?"

I sighed. "My new ride."

"You jest."

"We can't all ask Daddy for a brand-new convertible," I bristled.

"Please don't tell me you're going to actually be seen in this?"

"It's either this or walk everywhere."

"I'd start walking, sweetie. At least you can wear cute shoes."

"Please. Like you'd ever walk anywhere except the red carpet. Anyway, I'd rather drive a tacky car than spend my life as a high-maintenance label whore."

She turned and yelled toward the apartment. "Coelle! Get out here! You *have* to see this!"

Danny leaned over, kissed my cheek, and said loyally, "Well, I like it. It'll stand out from all the boring European sedans choking up the freeways."

Jacinda laughed. "You're only saying that because you're hoping to get lucky in the backseat."

Danny grinned. "Maybe."

I covered my face in my hands. "My whole life just sucks."

"What's going on?" Coelle joined us on the sidewalk, all dolled up in diamond earrings, a silver minidress, and silver sandals with straps that snaked halfway up her calves.

Aside from her scenes on *Twilight's Tempest*, I'd never seen her out of sweats and jeans. "Hey, Ms. Hilton! Where's the party?"

"Oh, this?" She tugged the hem of her dress down. "I'm going to some charity auction dinner thing with Quentin tonight and I'm supposed to dress young, sexy, and fun." She looked grim. "What's all the yelling about?"

"That." Jacinda pointed out the ginormous van casting a dark shadow on the sidewalk.

Coelle gave it a cursory once-over. "Looks like a giant goose. So?"

Jacinda dissolved into giggles. "The Goose! That's perfect! I love it!"

"I have no roommates," I told them. "You're dead to me."

"That's Eva's new car," Danny explained to the mystified Coelle.

"For real?" The look she gave me this time was even more pitying than the one she'd given me when she told me my father was dead. "God, I'm sorry, Eva. Is Laurel punishing you again?"

I glared at her. "No, no one's punishing me. You know, outside of the three-one-oh area code, people would kill for a car like this."

"If you say so." She turned to Jacinda, who was still cracking up. "I couldn't book a makeup artist on such short notice, so I need you to do my eyes, okay?"

"Can't." Jacinda gasped for breath. "I've been blinded by the sheer hideousness of the Goose."

"That's what they're going to call it from now on," I moaned to Danny as my roommates trooped back toward the apartment.

He tried to keep a straight face. "Honestly, it's not that bad."

"Not that bad? It's the kind of van serial killers use to pick up unsuspecting victims! There's no windows in the back!"

He moved in for a kiss. "I'm thinking we could use that to our advantage."

But I blocked him, pressing my index finger against his lips. "I'm so not in the mood for this. First my dad's dead, then my aunt has to be bludgeoned into telling me about him, now I'm stuck driving this death trap, and you just want to make out."

"I'm trying to see the glass as half-full." He threw an arm

around my shoulder, sabotaging my attempts to freeze him out. "You know what you need?"

"A chocolate truffle as big as my head and a guest spot on *Pimp My Ride*?"

"You need to go to dinner with me. We'll drive out to Santa Monica, watch the sun set, sit out on the beach . . ."

The sinking sun and the sharp, salty breeze did sound tempting, but I shook my head. "I just want to be by myself tonight. To think about what I'm going to say to my mom tomorrow."

"Want me to come with you to see her? I could skip my bio lab."

"Thanks, but no. I have to do this alone."

This time he was the one who pulled away. "You want to do everything alone. What do you need me for?"

"Lots of things." I turned around and took off his baseball cap. "Like this." I went up on tiptoe and kissed him. "And this." I kissed him again. Just as he started to slide his arms around my waist, we were interrupted by a loud, phlegmy cough.

"Oh, pardon me." Bissy Billington, former Miss Sweet Sixteen of the great state of Texas and the girl I'd inadvertently beat out for my first national commercial, cleared her throat a few more times. "I didn't mean to intrude on y'all's romantic interlude."

I sighed, handing Danny his hat back. "Can I help you, Bissy?"

As always, she was wearing white from top to toe, complete with a shiny white ribbon around her ponytail. "I wanted to let you know that your aunt got me a Diet Coke audition tomorrow, so if you're planning on throwing your fancy Hollywood connections around and doin' your little Beyonce routine, tell me in advance so I don't waste an afternoon."

"For the last time, I am sorry about the Samba commercial," I said wearily. "But it wasn't my fault! You saw what happened, I was only—"

"Save it, ya backstabbing little booty bandit!" She stamped one of her pristine white cowboy boots. "You think I'm just some dumb, backwoods hick, don't you? But you'll be sorry; no one steals a role from Belinda Jane Billington and lives to tell the tale! I'll get you back if it's the last thing I do."

"Belinda Jane," I mused. "That's your real name? And you voluntarily went with Bissy?"

Danny stepped into the catfight and offered up a handshake. "Hi. I'm Danny Bristow, Eva's boyfriend."

Okay. I know it's stupid, but my insides went all melty and fluttery when he introduced himself like that.

Bissy stopped glaring and regarded him speculatively. "Wasn't she supposed to be dating your stepbrother? And then she cheated on him with you?"

He stopped smiling and dropped his hand. "No. That is not what happened—"

"You better watch her like a hawk," Bissy advised. "She's a lying, backstabbing little vixen who'll stop at nothing to get what she wants."

"Aw, you're sweet," I drawled. "No one's ever called me a vixen before."

"Well, I got my eye on you," Bissy shot back. "You'll screw

up sooner or later and when you do, I'll be right there to take you down! Momma says—"

"Eva!" Coelle came rushing back to the sidewalk, mussing her freshly blow-dried hair in her haste. "Some psycho guy is at the door! He says he's looking for you!"

Danny looked at me questioningly, but all I could do was shrug. "Apparently word has spread about my vixen ways."

"Apparently." Coelle's eyes widened. "He says he's your soul mate! And he's got a ring!"

4

"No way." My jaw hit the ground when I saw the tall, bushy-haired figure standing at our door. *"No way."*

When Coelle had described the mystery visitor as "psycho," many possibilities had flashed through my imagination. Like a practical joke orchestrated by Bissy. An escaped inmate who had seen my Samba commercial one too many times. Orlando Bloom finally coming to his senses.

But I was completely unprepared for the reality: Jeff Oerte.

"What the hell are you doing here?" Seeing as he was my oldest friend from my hometown in Massachusetts, I probably should have given him a hug or asked him how he'd been.

But I was too flabbergasted to do anything more than stand and gawk.

"Spring break," he said, as if this explained everything. "I've come out to win you over." And with that, he dropped to one knee on our woven straw welcome mat and produced a black velvet box from the pocket of his baggy cargo khakis.

I repeat, he was my oldest friend from Massachusetts. *Friend.* My gaze ricocheted from Danny to Coelle to Jeff. "I . . . you . . . *huh?*"

He popped open the top of the box to reveal a slim gold band with a tiny chip of what appeared to be blue topaz in the center. "I'm here to do what I should have done last summer."

Jacinda popped her head out from the living room.

"Is he proposing?" She appraised the ring with a mercenary smirk. "Don't accept that. It looks like he found it in a gumball machine. Hold out for at least a carat and a half. Flawless."

"Holy crap, you're *proposing?*" Coelle stumbled on one of her spindly silver heels. "She's only eighteen!"

"You're proposing to my girlfriend?" Danny sounded more incredulous than angry. "Right in front of me?"

"Could you all just shut up for a minute?" I put my hands on my hips. "Calm down. No one's proposing to anybody!" I turned to Jeff. "Right? What's going on?"

"What does it look like? I'm asking you to . . . you know!" He winced as the rough fibers of the welcome mat dug into his knee. "Look? I have a ring and everything!"

I turned to Danny. "Is Ashton Kutcher about to pop out of the bushes? Because, ha ha, you guys really got me good."

But no one was laughing. Jeff continued waving the ring under my nose. "Come on. We were meant to be together. I can't waste any more time."

Some distant, analytical voice in my head was insisting that this was a grand romantic gesture, the kind of sweep-me-off-my-feet move that all girls fantasized about. Who wouldn't melt into a sweet, sticky puddle of syrup at the prospect of a surprise ring and an impassioned declaration of love?

Well, me, for starters. Maybe I just wasn't the romantic type. Maybe I was a heartless, frigid shell of a human.

Or maybe there's nothing worse than the grand romantic gesture from the wrong guy.

I squinted at Jeff, trying to figure out what had changed about him over the last few months. Same unruly sandy blond hair, same puckish blue eyes, same long, lanky frame. But there was definitely a disturbance in the Force.

"Since when are you interested in winning me over?" I asked.

He struggled to his feet, nodding at Danny. "Are you the so-called boyfriend?"

Danny drew himself up to his full height; even though he was six feet, he couldn't match Jeff's six feet, three inches. "I'm her for-real boyfriend."

"Well, I'm here to take her away from you. Nothing personal. We're destined to be together, so I'm going to have to ask you to step aside."

"You kids from the Berkshires are *messed up*," Jacinda declared.

"Guys . . ." I tried to take charge. "Can we please take this inside? We're making a scene."

"A really juicy one." Jacinda sounded ready to pop some corn and sell tickets.

I pointed at the door. "Everybody in."

We filed into the living room, where Coelle and Jacinda perched on the sofa, Jeff sat on the edge of the coffee table, and Danny remained standing next to me with a proprietary hand on my neck.

"Don't worry," I murmured to him. "This is all a huge misunderstanding."

"What's to misunderstand? This guy shows up with a ring and claims he's going to 'take' you from me. I'd say we're crystal clear."

"Okay." I shook my head and tried to start from the beginning. "This is Jeff Oerte, my next-door neighbor from Alden. We've been friends since kindergarten. He's like my brother."

"Not anymore," Jeff corrected.

"What is the matter with you?" I hissed at him. "What are you *doing*?"

"I told you." Jeff pulled out the ring box again. "We're meant to be together."

"Um, I beg to differ." My voice came out hoarse and hysterical, but I think I could be excused for freaking out under the circumstances. "I'm eighteen years old, I'm dating somebody else, and I'm not ready to marry anyone. Neither are you!"

"We could have a long engagement."

"What, ten years?"

"If that's what it takes."

"Come on. If I said 'yes' and put that ring on my finger, you would hyperventilate and pass out."

"I would not!" Jeff protested.

"You couldn't even ask Callie Kwitowski to go to the movies without throwing up twice before homeroom!"

"That was last year," he said witheringly. "I've matured a lot since then."

"And you're proving that by stealth bombing me with a ring when you know I've got a boyfriend?"

"That's right." The tips of his ears turned bright red. "I'm a man now. I see what I want, I go after it."

Jacinda whipped a Kit Kat out of her purse and offered a piece to Coelle (who, of course, refused), both of them transfixed by the drama unfolding in front of them.

Danny's expression hovered somewhere between confusion and outrage. "So you guys never actually dated in high school?"

"No," I said firmly. "Jeff, back me up on this one."

"No," he muttered.

"We're just friends. I don't know where this is all coming from."

"Yes, you do!" Jeff insisted. "I asked you to homecoming!"

"Yeah, and then there was the whole scandal with Bryan Dufort and you didn't speak to me for three months!"

"How many times do I have to apologize for that? I admit I was wrong! I'll never not speak to you for three months again."

"Who's Bryan Dufort?" Danny wanted to know.

Jeff's eyebrows shot up. "You didn't tell him?"

"Tell me what?" Danny asked.

"Nothing." I gave Jeff a warning glare. "Listen to me. This whole thing is crazy. We are friends. That is it."

"You'll come around." He nodded. "I know you better than anyone in the world."

"True," I admitted. "But my whole life is changing. I have new friends, new career interests, a new boyfriend . . ."

"Him?" Jeff regarded Danny with arrogant amusement. "He can't compete with me. He doesn't even know about Bryan Dufort."

Jacinda's Kit Kat wrapper crinkled as she broke off a new segment.

"Leave Bryan Dufort out of this! You're my best friend and I love you, and that ring is just"—I swallowed hard—"stunning. But you can't show up in Los Angeles without calling and expect me to suddenly fall in love with you."

"Sure I can." Jeff seemed totally unfazed by our spellbound audience. "Oh, and listen. I'm staying till next Sunday and I kind of need a place to stay, so is it okay if I crash here?"

I bit my lip and looked at my roommates. "Well . . ."

"No." Danny glowered at him.

"Then where am I supposed to sleep?" Jeff demanded.

Coelle finally spoke up, calm and practical. "Quentin just moved into a new condo on Crescent Heights and he has an extra bedroom. If you're willing to help him paint and chip in for a few pizzas, you might be able to stay there."

Danny turned to me. "Who's Quentin?"

"Her new boyfriend. Sort of."

"My photo-op boyfriend," Coelle clarified.

Jacinda stuck out her lower lip. "I can't believe I'm the only one *not* having man problems today. Must be a sign of the apocalypse."

"Want to have dinner tonight?" Jeff asked me hopefully.

"NO!" My last shred of self-control snapped. "I don't want to have dinner! All I want is five minutes of peace and quiet to grieve my dead father! Now get out, all of you! Get out, get out, get out!"

"Her father's dead?" Jeff whispered to Jacinda. "I thought she didn't have a father?"

"Epic tear-jerker saga," Jacinda whispered back. "I'll tell you the whole thing later. Don't worry, she's just cranky because she has to drive the Goose."

"Get out!" I shrieked.

"I live here!" Jacinda shrieked back.

"Stop baiting her," Coelle admonished, shooing Jacinda and Jeff toward the stairs. "Let's go. Jacinda, you finish my eyes and Jeff, I'll call Quentin and ask if he'll let you stay there for a few days."

Once they cleared out, I tried to unclench my fists and slow my racing, ragged breaths.

After a long pause, Danny spoke up. "Do I have to get out, too?"

I shook my head and let him enfold me in a hug.

"You okay?" he asked.

I nodded.

"You still want to be alone tonight?"

I nodded.

"You're not just saying that to get rid of me so you can pick up where you left off with crazy ring boy?"

I finally smiled. "Shut up. He's not crazy. He's sweet. He's just . . . not the right guy."

He kissed the top of my head. "Am I the right guy?"

I shrugged one shoulder, but kept smiling.

"So if I show up with a ring someday, you're not going to callously reject me?"

"There's only one way to find out."

"Come in!" my mom called from inside the ivy-covered stucco walls of Laurel's poolside *casita*. "Door's open!"

I kept right on knocking. I was her guest, not to mention her daughter. She could get off her perfect supermodel ass and open the door.

"I said, *come in*!" Her voice took on an edge of whiny irritation. "You have opposable thumbs; use 'em!"

I was starting to remember why our last confrontation had gone so badly. My mother couldn't even take a shower or brush her teeth without drenching the whole affair in melodrama. Intellectually, I knew that I shouldn't get sucked into passive-aggressive mind games with a woman who was certifiably insane, but still, I hung back on the welcome mat, waiting.

And waiting.

And waiting.

Argh. Swearing under my breath, I accepted defeat and let myself in. Laurel's guesthouse was decorated in the same style as her mansion—lots of dark wood, white fabric, and natural light pouring through the floor-to-ceiling windows—but unlike the mansion, the *casita* had no housekeeper to pick up after the occupant. Though my mother hadn't strutted down a catwalk in at least a decade, the casual sloppiness she'd developed while living out of suitcases in luxury hotels around the world had stayed with her. The sitting room looked like . . . well, it looked like our living room, actually, after Jacinda returned from one of her shopping sprees. Inside-out clothes and damp towels were draped over lampshades and end tables, shoes and Zone bar wrappers were scattered all over the beige carpet, and the open door to the bedroom revealed an unmade bed and a trail of abandoned lipstick and mascara tubes.

"Mom?" I crossed the sitting room and peeked into the bedroom, a little apprehensive about what I'd find, considering what had happened the last time she'd "welcomed" me into her home. But the room was empty except for rumpled white linens and the distinct smell of rum.

Great. She'd already started drinking. That always brought a whole new level of heartwarming intimacy to these little mother-daughter chats.

"Mom?" I upped the volume this time, but she didn't answer. Then I heard a muted clink and a splash from the direction of the bathroom.

"Hello?" I tapped on the bathroom door. "Mom, I'm here. Didn't Aunt Laurel tell you I was coming over?"

"Of course, baby girl. Come on in." Her voice, now sweet and lilting, echoed off the tiled walls.

I cleared my throat. "I'll just wait out here until you're done."

"Don't be silly, darling. I'm soaking in the tub and I'll be in here for at least another hour." The clinking got louder. Ice against a glass tumbler.

I cracked open the door. "What are you drinking in there?"

"A bubble bath isn't really complete without a mojito. Want one?"

Most of my friends would have killed for a mom like this: the fun mom. The party mom. The mom who offers her eighteen-year-old a mojito just for the hell of it. Well, they could have her.

"No, I do not want a mojito," I said sternly, trying to set a good example for her. She'd been to rehab for narcotics in the eighties—she should know better than to swill cocktails in the bathtub all by herself. "I'm coming in. Cover yourself with bubbles."

When I entered the bathroom, she was immersed in a huge white bathtub, splashing the floral-scented water with a cigarette in one hand and a glass filled with fizzy greenish liquid in the other. Her long brunette hair was twisted up into a damp topknot, her big golden eyes looked glassy, and her long limbs were splayed out with total disregard for modesty.

I glanced at the bottle of Bacardi on the glass shelf above the tub and asked, "How long have you been in here?"

"Awhile."

"How much have you had to drink?"

"Not that much. Could you be a lamb and grab the champagne chilling in the fridge? There's a bottle of Perrier Jouët on the top shelf."

"Does Laurel know you raided her wet bar?"

"Who cares? It's not like she's ever gonna drink it," Mom countered. "She's never even home. Someone might as well enjoy it."

Ladies and gentlemen, the amazing Marisela Cordes. No matter how tipsy she got, her powers of rationalization remained superb.

"You've spent the whole afternoon in the tub getting drunk, haven't you?" I couldn't hide my disgust. "You knew I was coming over to talk about my dad and *this* is how you get ready?"

"A bottle of rum and two packs of cigarettes are the only way I've ever been able to deal with Anatole Farnsworth," she snapped. "By the time we're done here, you'll want to throw back a few shots yourself. So spare me the lecture."

"Sorry to traumatize you with my existence," I snitted. "I didn't ask to be born, you know."

"Neither did I." She took a long, desperate drag on her cigarette, then ashed on the white tile floor. "Now stop with the flinty-eyed accusations and get me my goddamn champagne."

If I didn't comply, she'd slosh out of that tub and go for the fridge herself, wet, naked, and probably slipping on the tile floor and breaking her neck. So I stalked back out to the kitchenette and retrieved the chilled green bottle, figuring that at least it'd be easier to get answers out of her if she were smashed.

"Here." I handed her the bottle and a coffee mug I'd just rinsed out in the sink. "How was Scottsdale?"

"Very healing," she said with a straight face. "I feel completely centered now; got my priorities all sorted out." She peeled back the gold foil and popped the cork, which elicited a high-pitched bark from the bedroom. "Oh, shut it, Rhett."

I sat down on the closed toilet lid and drew my feet up in alarm. "Rhett's in here?"

"Of course. I dog-sit him whenever Laurel can't take him to her office."

Right on cue, the world's cutest little black poodle trotted into the bathroom, nails clicking on the tile. He was dragging a bejeweled silver flip-flop in his mouth and growling at the champagne cork.

"That little beast is a menace," I said as Rhett halted his pursuit of the cork long enough to lunge at my pant legs.

"Don't be silly. He's adorable." She glanced at the mangled flip-flop and giggled.

"He's only adorable because that's not your shoe."

"True. Don't tell Laurel I borrowed her new Giuseppe

Zanottis, okay? Ooh, speaking of which, I like your earrings. Can I try them on for a sec?"

Without a word, I unhooked the dangly threadthroughs from my earlobes and handed them to her. Luckily, they were only silver, not gold. I'd learned long ago not to wear anything I valued around her. She had a way of appropriating other people's property.

She worked the silver strands into her own ears and twisted her head to admire her reflection in the bathtub faucet. "Cute," she decreed. "Very cute. You don't mind if I hang on to these for a few days, do you?"

"Do whatever you want." Keeping a wary eye on Rhett, who was tugging the fluffy white towels off the rack and fashioning a nest for himself on the floor, I returned to the business at hand. "I want to talk about my dad."

She grimaced, then submerged her entire head underwater. From the profusion of bubbles roiling the surface near her topknot, I guessed she was screaming under there.

Just when I was starting to wonder if she'd really prefer drowning herself to discussing my parentage, she jerked her head up, sputtering and swiping at her face with the hand that held her cigarette.

"Careful," I said. "You'll burn your eye out."

"You *had* to go snooping through Laurel's study, didn't you? You couldn't leave well enough alone?"

I shrugged. "Nope."

"I tried to protect you." She shook her head to one side, trying to rid her ear of water while still hanging on to her smoke. Rhett curled his lip as a few droplets of water landed on his paw. "When this is all over and you wish you never heard the name Anatole Farnsworth, don't tell me I didn't warn you." She slammed her drained mojito glass down on the shelf, grabbed the champagne and poured a big mugful. "Here's what you need to know: Anatole Farnsworth was a lying, cheating, career-ruining rat bastard."

I kept my tone even. "And yet you liked him enough to have a child with him."

"He said he needed me. He said he was going to leave his wife and marry me. He said he was going to take care of you and give you the kind of life I'd always wanted for my child. But when I had you, he sent his lawyers to tell me that he'd *sue* if I put his name on the birth certificate. He destroyed my reputation, he blackballed me in Hollywood, and then, just to top it all off, he *died*."

"On the tennis court, Aunt Laurel said."

"Yeah. While he was screaming at his partner about a double fault." She looked pleased about this. "I told him he needed to eat better and stop smoking those vile cigars, but would he listen? Nooo." She paused to gulp her booze and light a fresh Virginia Slim.

"Well . . ." Maybe Coelle and Jacinda and Laurel had been right. Maybe I *didn't* want to know these things about my own father. "Why did you hook up with him if he was so horrible?"

"Because I was in love." Her eyes softened. "And he was,

too. In the beginning, anyway. But then one thing led to another and next thing I knew, I had attorneys in the delivery room threatening to litigate."

I reached over, snatched up the bottle of Perrier Jouët, and swigged.

"See? I told you you'd need a drink for this conversation." She exhaled slowly, her head lolling back against the tub's porcelain rim. "I started going out with him because I was flattered that a studio head would pay attention to me. Plus, I had just done my first *Vogue* cover and I was trying to break into acting, and sleeping with him seemed like a great career move."

I took another bracing slug of champagne.

"He did everything he could to win me over—flew me to Napa and Santa Barbara and started giving me all this jewelry . . . I just lost my head. You know me, always the hopeless romantic."

Hopeless is right. But I shut up and let her ramble. With any luck, I'd find the kernel of truth at the bottom of all this bitterness.

"Evie, I made the dumbest mistake a girl can make: I believed him when he said he was going to leave his wife." She pointed her cigarette at me. "Don't believe a man when he says that, no matter how sincere he seems. There's a life lesson for you."

I pretended to scribble this down on an imaginary notepad.

"Laurel kept telling me that he would never marry me and that I should just dump him before things went sour. But I was young and I didn't really understand who his wife is in Hollywood and I just—"

"Hang on." I dredged up the printed obituary announcement, which was torn and dog-eared by this time, and consulted it. "Daphne Holloway? Who is she?"

My mother's eyes narrowed to glittering, murderous slits. "Daphne Holloway Farnsworth. The catty bitch behind the rat bastard. She's the reason Anatole was able to backstab his way up the studio system. He was a tough, ruthless SOB, but he came from nothing. Daphne was old Hollywood money— he married her for her family connections and her trust fund. He didn't love her. The truth about your father is that he only cared about three things: money, power, and himself."

I studied my cuticles and tried to tamp down my surging emotions. "That's a beautiful story."

"Well, you wanted to know, didn't you? You couldn't just let it lie. And how do you think I've felt all this time, watching you demonize me and idolize your father?"

"How do you think *I* feel?" I shot back. "Knowing that he only wanted your body, you only wanted his money, and neither of you wanted me?"

She hurled the empty mojito glass across the room, where it shattered against the tile. Rhett cowered, then bolted out the door. *"How dare you?"*

"What? That's the truth, isn't it?"

Predictably, she crumpled and started to cry. "Is that what you think of me?"

"What else am I supposed to think?" I demanded. "You just said—"

"Don't you sit there and judge me! You have no idea what—"

"Oh, and by the way, do I have a sister or a brother or what?" I nodded at her shock. "Yeah. I found out about the other pregnancy. What'd you do, Mom? Abort my sister? Dump her on someone else to raise, just like you dumped me? What?"

Her face went ashen.

"Mom?" I stopped screaming because her expression was starting to freak me out. "Hello?"

"I can't . . ." She started to shake, her eyes shut tight. "You were never supposed to find out about any of this!"

"If one more person says that, I swear to God . . ."

"Go away!" She broke into sobs, dropping her cigarette into the water and burying her face in her hands. "Just leave me alone."

I sighed. "I know you're upset, but you have to—"

"Stop talking! Get out!"

"Mom. Calm down. I just want to know about the other baby, okay?"

Choking, soul-wracking sobs were my only reply.

I retreated to the sitting room and waited on the couch until the wailing subsided. Even Rhett looked worried. He stopped destroying everything in his path and cast anxious looks at the bathroom door.

Five minutes after she lapsed into silence, I started to worry. "Mom? Are you okay?"

When I eased open the door, I found her slumped back

against the tub, slackjawed and asleep (okay, passed out), with mascara smeared all over her cheeks. Luckily, she hadn't drowned yet, so I drained the tub, covered her with towels, and swept up the pieces of shattered glass before I left.

A good daughter would have left a big bottle of water and a few Advils by the tub to help her nurse the impending hangover, but I wasn't a good daughter. I was just the product of all her lust and excess and constant need for more, more, more.

After I let myself out of the *casita,* I read the obituary one more time. *Survived by three sons.* My half brothers. What were they like? Did they look like me?

Instead of heading for the Goose, I made a detour to the main house. Time to call in a favor from Aunt Laurel.

5

"No." Laurel smacked her open palm on the white linen tablecloth, causing the lit candle in the center of the restaurant table to flicker. "No. A thousand times no."

"They're my flesh and blood," I argued. "I have a right to meet them. They have a right to meet me!"

Her lips curled up in a humorless smile. "Trust me, pet, they don't want to meet you. And for God's sake, keep your voice down. There's a table full of Warner Brothers V.P.s over there trying to enjoy their appetizers in peace."

When I'd shown up on her doorstep and demanded a sit-down with my half brothers, Laurel had announced she was taking me out to dinner. Presumably because I couldn't scream and yell and carry on in a swanky restaurant the way I could in her dining room. So we'd decamped for Sojo, Laurel's new favorite spot for Indo-European fusion. She dropped by for dinner so often, the hostess knew her by name and asked after Rhett.

"How do you know they don't want to meet me?" Flushed with frustration, I peeled off my wool cardigan and draped it over the back of my chair. "What if they don't even know I exist? What if no one ever told them about their dad and my mom?"

The smug smile vanished, and I knew I had gotten close to the truth.

"They don't know, do they?"

"I have no idea." She straightened her shoulders, taking on the same air of emotional Teflon she displayed at her office. "Daphne knew about your mother—she'd hired a PI to track Anatole's affairs so she'd have leverage in the event of a divorce—but I can't imagine she'd tell her children."

"So?" I did a little table pounding myself. "They have no idea they have a half sister living right in the same city."

She paused, furrowing her brow and puckering her lips.

"What?" I demanded.

"I'm trying to decide how best to say this."

"Just come out with it," I exhorted. "Stop treating me like I'm five."

"Fair enough." She waved off the approaching waiter and adjusted her starched white shirt collar. "While Daphne's children are, technically speaking, related to you, I don't think you should get your hopes up about getting all bondy with them. For one thing, they're a lot older than you. They're probably in their mid-to-late thirties by now. At least."

"So they're old. Good. They can buy me beer."

"Then there's the matter of money. When Anatole died, he left behind a sizable estate. Stocks, art, real estate, you name it."

"Okay, so they're old and rich," I agreed impatiently. "So what?"

"So they're probably not going to be too thrilled at the prospect of sharing the wealth with a surprise illegitimate sister who shows up on their doorstep with no warning."

Leave it to my aunt to always see the bottom line in terms of cold, hard cash. "Give me a break. I don't want their money."

She arched one eyebrow. "I know that. But *they* don't. And there's no one more suspicious and greedy than a trust-fund baby who didn't earn his inheritance."

I sat back in my chair and gave her the same kind of steely look she probably gave to studio execs when she was about to walk away from a deal. "So what are you saying here?"

"I'm saying that maybe there's a reason none of the Farnsworths ever came looking for you. Maybe your mom knew exactly what she was doing when she took you out of Hollywood."

Right. The woman who was currently naked and unconscious in the bathtub with a foul mixture of rum and champagne on her breath. "Yeah, Mom's the original mastermind."

Laurel caught the eye of a waiter across the room and beckoned him over. "Mari screwed up her own life and she was determined not to let the same thing happen to you. She had your best interests at heart when she took you to Massachusetts."

"Don't even start with that. She dropped me off with Grandma and Grandpa when I was three so she could spend the next fifteen years partying her way around the world and not returning any of my phone calls."

"She wanted to protect you from Hollywood and everything that went with it."

"And yet, here I am." I spread my arms wide. "Somehow managing to survive in the big, bad city."

She opened her menu and threw a wide, fake smile at the approaching waiter. "Steer clear of the Farnsworths. All of them. That's my final word on the matter."

"Well, it's not your decision to make." I crossed my arms. "It's mine. And I want to meet my family. Which brings me to my next topic: Mom's other baby."

"Oops, time to order!" She leaned forward and started asking our waiter inane questions about plum sauce and ahi tuna.

"And for you?" The waiter turned to me. Despite my pissy mood, I couldn't help noticing he was scorching hot, even by Los Angeles standards.

I glared at my aunt. "I'm going to need a few minutes."

"Of course." He beat a hasty retreat for the kitchen.

As soon as he was out of earshot, my aunt rounded on me

with tight-lipped fury. "Listen, pet. I don't care how petulant you feel, you do not treat waiters that way. I have a reputation to uphold in this town, and I will not be known as the agent who reps snotty little brats."

"I wasn't being rude to him," I pointed out. "I was being rude to you."

"That's it." She jabbed the air with her salad fork. "No dessert for you."

I was dying to ask if she was going to put me in time-out, too, but decided I had pushed her far enough for one evening. "Hey, did you see that guy's name tag?"

"Who?" She frowned. "The waiter?"

"Yeah. His name's Gavin."

She looked puzzled. "And . . . ?"

"Do you think he's the same guy that waited on us at Kate Mantilini? The day I first got here?"

"If he works at Kate Mantilini, how could he work here?"

"Maybe he switched jobs," I suggested. "I mean, how many chiseled, blond surfer guys named Gavin could there be?"

"I haven't the slightest. But if you're such a big fan of his, try being a little nicer next time he asks to take your order."

"Fine. Now will you help me meet my half brothers or not?"

She exhaled loudly. "The Farnsworths are not the Bradys, pet. You're hoping for a fairy tale, but you're going to get V.C. Andrews."

I glared at her. "I want. To meet them."

"You are so stubborn."

"I learned it from watching you."

"Fair point. All right." She relented. "I'll make a few calls, try to set up a lunch. But I can't promise anything."

"So how'd it go with your mom?" Jacinda asked when I returned to our apartment. She was sprawled out on the living room carpet, flipping through a stack of fashion magazines while clad in a black cashmere sweater, frilly red panties and fleece-lined suede slippers that looked like they used to belong to a fifty-year-old history professor.

"She cried and threw stuff and passed out in the bathtub." I closed the door behind me. "Same old, same old."

"She passed out?" Jacinda looked up from a layout on bikinis and sundresses. "In the water?"

"Oh, relax, I drained the tub before I left."

"What a humanitarian."

"Yeah, I'm on the short list for the Nobel Peace Prize." I flung myself down next to her and nodded at the huge bunch of pink carnations on the coffee table. "What's this?"

"Those are for you."

I clapped both hands over my heart. "Aw. That is *so* sweet."

She made a face like I'd just mentioned "outlet sale" or "off-the-rack." "Carnations? Honey, those are the fake Rolex of flowers."

"I know, but who cares? Danny's a full-time student. He doesn't have a lot of money and besides—"

She cut me off with, "Oh, these aren't from Danny. They're from Jeff."

I stopped gushing about how it was the thought that counted. "Jeff?"

"Mm-hmm." She went back to studying cruisewear trends. "Coelle convinced Quentin to take him in for a few days, and he wanted to continue the lovefest. He said they were your favorite flower. Frankly, I expected a lot better from you. But I guess the old saying is true: you can take a girl out of a backwoods hick town, but you can't take the backwoods hick town out of—"

"They are not my favorite flower!" I insisted. "Not since I was eleven, anyway. I don't know where he comes up with this stuff."

She turned the page and sniffed idly at a perfume sample. "I told him to send something classier, but would he listen? Nooo . . ."

"You tried to tell him?" I snatched the magazine away from her. "You encouraged him to do this?"

"Sure. He's sort of cute, in a doofy way. Besides, I'm utterly bored; we need a little excitement around here."

"That's it. You need a new boyfriend," I decided. "Right now."

"Amen, sister." Her hair pooled in a blonde halo around her head as she rolled onto her back. "But I'm sick to death of L.A. men. Maybe I can get a role in a movie that's filming on location. Like Vancouver. Or Australia. Those Aussie guys are hot."

"Send me a postcard from Sydney," I told her. "And stay out of my love life."

"I'll try." She moved on to the next magazine in her stash. "But can I just point out one thing?"

"No."

"As gag-worthy as carnations are, at least Jeff sent you flowers. What has Danny done for you lately?"

I tossed my head. "Danny has been a rock. An anchor. A . . . a paragon of dependability."

"A rock? That's it? Eva, there'll be plenty of time for quiet desperation when you're thirty. Right now? You need to *live*."

"Spoken like a girl who's never had any real problems in her life."

"You're not gonna be eighteen forever. This is your only chance to be young and free. You need to live it up. Bad boys." She shot me a pointed look. "Hot sex."

"I'm going to have hot sex," I protested.

"Not with Danny, you're not." She clicked her tongue at me. "And the sad thing is, at the rate you're going, you'll never know the difference. Then one day you'll wake up, a frumpy soccer mom with two-point-five kids and some balding accountant husband in the suburbs. And you'll never experience raw, unbridled passion."

I wrinkled my nose. "Like you have?"

"Hey, which one of us is woman enough to wear the leather thong?"

Keys jangled in the lock, saving me from having to come up with an appropriately stinging response to that.

"Hi." Coelle stuck her head in to assess the situation in the living room. "I come bearing boys." She glanced pointedly at Jacinda's outfit. "Do you want to put something on before I bring them inside?"

"Why?" Jacinda rolled back over onto her stomach, her sweater riding up even higher. "Let 'em in."

Coelle ushered in Jeff and Quentin, both boys sporting recent sunburns and way too much hair gel.

Jeff made a beeline for me, stepping right over Jacinda's seminude body. "Like your flowers?" he asked, taking a seat and draping his arm over the back of the sofa.

"Who *are* you?" I whispered, craning forward so he wouldn't get the mistaken impression that I welcomed his physical overtures.

"I'm your former best friend and future boyfriend."

"Wrong," I told him.

"Right."

"Why is your face all red and peeling?"

"Quentin just got this killer Porsche convertible and we spent all afternoon breaking it in on the PCH—that's the Pacific Coast Highway."

"I know what the PCH is. But apparently, you need someone to tell you about SPF." I jerked my head toward the carnations. "We have to talk about this."

He smiled. "Good."

"No, Jeff, *not* good. What am I supposed to tell Danny?"

His cocky smile faltered. For the first time since he'd arrived, I caught a glimpse of the real Jeff Oerte—the Jeff I'd known and loved (platonically!) all these years. "I don't know. Can't you stop obsessing over that guy for one second?"

Coelle stepped in between us, smiling hopefully. "My publicist scored six invites to the *Buzzkill* afterparty tonight. So we can all go, plus Danny. Who's up for a triple date?"

6

"*Why* is he here, again?" Danny stared at Jeff, who was trying to talk the VIP room's bartender out of a shot of whiskey (unsuccessfully, based on the bartender's sneer). "He just got off the plane yesterday. How is he best friends with Coelle's photo-op boyfriend already?"

"I know it's annoying, but don't let it ruin our night. Pretend he's not here." I snuggled closer to him on the velvet banquette and squeezed his upper arm through his crisp blue shirt. And then squeezed again. "Ooh, someone's been hitting the weight room extra hard."

"Season starts at the end of the month," he reminded me. "My elbow's almost a hundred percent again and Coach said that a scout might drop by one of the games next week, so I'm trying to get in some extra workouts."

"A scout?" I stopped focusing on the carnation-sending party crasher for a second. "What kind of scout?"

"You know, for the majors."

He'd gotten a baseball scholarship to UCLA, but I hadn't realized that he was major-league material. "They recruit pitchers who are still in college?"

"Depends on how good you are and what kind of draft number you're looking at." He took a sip of Coke (no alcohol allowed during training) and squeezed me back. "Sports agents are always looking for the next big thing. Kerry Wood signed with the Cubs when he was still in high school."

"Yeah, but . . ." I frowned at him. "You're going to leave me and sign with the Cubs?"

"Only if I'm really lucky." He laughed as I pretended to pout. "Don't worry, no one's asking me to sign anything yet. I haven't even talked to an agent."

"But . . ." I stuck out my lower lip. "The scout."

"Even if I did move to Chicago, I'd fly you out every weekend. Swear to God."

"First class," I warned.

"Deal."

"Well . . ." I pretended to deliberate. "I don't know. I'm not sure I'm going to waste all my weekends on a guy who left me in L.A. for a chance to stand around on a mound of dirt, wearing ugly polyester pants on TV."

"Hey, you dance around in your underwear on TV," he reminded me. "You look great, by the way."

I'd managed to zip myself into one of Jacinda's leftovers—a flirty red strapless L.A.M.B. cocktail dress. Since I was about half a foot taller than her, the hem was short enough to raise a few eyebrows, but Danny seemed to be a big fan. He leaned in for a kiss and then . . .

"Hi, guys." Coelle collapsed next to us, clutching a sequined white purse in one hand and a glass of champagne in the other. "Can I hang out with you for a while? Now that we're past the press gauntlet, I don't have to deal with Quentin anymore."

Danny looked at me. I looked at him.

"Quentin seems like a nice guy," I urged. "You should give him a chance."

"Yeah, he's probably fascinating once you get past all the hair gel," Danny agreed.

"I guess." She shrugged, blithely ignoring our attempts to continue with our PDA. "There's nothing wrong with him, really, but he's all style, no substance."

"That would explain why Jacinda's been flipping her hair at him all night."

"Well, she's welcome to him." Coelle opened her evening bag and peered inside. "Assuming she can tear him away from Jeff."

"Yeah, what's the deal with those two?" Danny glanced over toward the bar, where Quentin had managed to obtain two drinks and was sharing his windfall with Jeff. "Are they long-lost brothers or what?"

She sipped her champagne. "Jeff likes to snowboard, Quentin likes to snowboard . . . it's a match made in manly man heaven. They're planning a trip to Big Bear next week."

"Good," Danny said. "Maybe Jeff'll start stalking your date instead of mine."

"Be fair. He's not *stalking* me," I admonished. "He just took an emotional wrong turn or something."

Coelle pulled a creased sheaf of papers out of her purse and said absently, "Is that how you explain the flowers?"

Danny stiffened. "What flowers?"

I shot Coelle a glare that would melt all the snow at Big Bear and said, "Nothing. It's no big deal."

He pulled away and demanded, "He sent you flowers?"

"Thanks a lot," I muttered to Coelle, before admitting to Danny, "If you want to get all technical about it, then yes, he did, but it was really Jacinda's idea and—"

"I can't believe this! Who the hell does he think he is?"

"He's harmless!" I insisted. "Just ignore him."

"The guy flew three thousand miles and showed up at your doorstep with a ring! I'm supposed to ignore that?"

"Well, no, but . . ." I shook my head impatiently. "I'm having lunch with him on Wednesday; we'll talk this whole thing out and he'll come to his senses. I know it's weird—believe me, as weird as this is for you, it's eight thousand times weirder for me—but he's one of my best friends. Try to have a little compassion."

"Sorry, but I can't dredge up any compassion for the jackass who's trying to steal my girlfriend."

"Try harder." I smiled. "You're the one I want. Not him. Nothing he can say or do or send me is going to change that."

"I guess," he grumbled.

"You're the one who'll get to see my racy new lingerie." This seemed to cheer him up. "See? Don't you feel sorry for him now?"

"No."

"Hey, I'll have to deal with all those slutty baseball groupies flinging themselves at you all season," I reminded him. "What do you call them? Cleat chasers?"

"The cleat chasers don't come with us to clubs on last-minute triple dates," he pointed out.

"Yeah, but as long as we trust each other, cleat chasers and crazy best friends won't matter. No one can come between us unless we let them, and we won't." I turned to Coelle, who had unfolded the papers from her bag and was studying them, oblivious to the dancing and drinking and high-profile schmoozing ensuing all around us. "Coelle? What are you doing?"

"Hmm?" She didn't look up.

"Hey. Little Miss Instigator. Any time you feel like jumping in here to explain that you and Quentin are not going to be bringing Jeff along every time you—oh my God, are those SAT words?" I craned my neck to get a better look at the pages in her hand.

She finally raised her head, blushing. "Yeah. Between the show and my fake relationship, I don't have enough time to study and I'm retaking the test on—"

"I don't care if you're retaking the test tomorrow morning at the crack of dawn! You are in a *club*! With brand-new sexy shoes and a very tasty date! There will be no SAT cramming!"

"I have to," she wailed as I confiscated her contraband crib sheets.

"You're going to have a mental breakdown if you keep this up," I declared, sounding eerily like Jacinda. "All your food rules, fashion rules, study rules . . . you need to relax. Take a little break."

She sulked for a few minutes, then headed back to join Jacinda and Quentin, who looked delighted to have two white-hot starlets hanging off his every word. Jeff laughed along with them but kept shooting glances over at me, which really put a damper on all the smooching with Danny, who ended up leaving early.

"I'll call you tomorrow," he promised as we waited for the valet to retrieve his car.

"Are you mad?" I asked, trying to discern his mood under the dizzying kaleidoscope of strobe lights and neon.

"No." He wouldn't quite meet my gaze. "But I have a midterm at eight thirty tomorrow and I have to finish studying."

"You and Coelle." I threw up my hands. "What am I going to do with you?"

"Wait till you start college—you'll feel my pain," he promised.

Wait till I started college. Which, presumably, I'd do at Leighton, back in Massachusetts, across the country from him. Might be time to check into the admission requirements at UCLA and USC.

"Don't worry about Jeff." I gave him the most seductive kiss in my repertoire as the valet chugged up in his ancient Mercedes.

He kissed me back, but didn't say anything, and by the time he got in the car and pulled away from the curb, his expression had gone from neutral to stormy.

Damn it! Last month C Money tried to scam on me, this month Jeff showed up out of the blue. . . . Why couldn't everyone just leave me alone and stop wrecking the best relationship I'd ever had? Why???

Well. I refused to be so easily defeated. This called for drastic action. I headed back into the club and charged up to Jacinda, who was giggling at one of Quentin's jokes and throwing back kir royales with wild abandon. "I need a favor," I announced. "Can I borrow your credit card?"

"I have you confirmed for an ocean-view suite on Saturday evening, Ms. Cordes," the hotel clerk chirped. "May I help you with anything else tonight?"

"No, thank you, that's it for me." I hung up my cellphone and turned to Jacinda, who had been listening to the conversation from across the kitchen, grinning her encouragement as I booked a suite at the Somerset, a hot new boutique hotel in Santa Monica.

We'd closed down the bar at the *Buzzkill* afterparty, finally convincing Coelle and Quentin that they should get some sleep before filming their big love scene for *Twilight's Tempest* tomorrow afternoon. Quentin might be nothing more than a photo-op boyfriend now, but I thought he had potential; Coelle really warmed up to him once I wrestled the SAT cheat sheet away. That girl could tear up the dance floor when she wanted to. She'd gone to bed while Jacinda and I changed into our PJs and plotted my next move with Danny.

"Thanks." I handed Jacinda's credit card back to her. "I'll pay you back as soon as I get my next residual check from Samba."

"Don't worry about it." She waved me off with the casual insouciance of a debutante whose family name regularly appeared in both the society and financial pages of the *New York Times*. Even now, slobbed out in white boxer shorts and a gigantic gray T-shirt she had stolen from an ex-boyfriend, you could practically see the tiara sparkling on her head.

"I mean it," I insisted. "I'm going to pay you back."

She shuddered. "Will you please stop talking about money? It's so vulgar. I don't care if you pay me back. Think of me as your sponsor on the road to womanhood."

I cupped one hand to my ear. "Are those violins I hear playing in the background?"

"Mock me and I'll downgrade you to a single room with a view of the parking garage," she threatened. "Now, let's get serious. You've got the guy—very cute, even if he is a little melba for my tastes—the hotel room . . ." She drummed her fingers on the chipped Formica countertop. "Time to move on to wardrobe. You never bought anything at Smoulder, did you?"

"No, I was too busy finding out about my dead dad."

"You are so ADD." She tsk-tsked me with her index finger. "You need to focus on what's really important in life. Let's go." She started up the stairs. "They have some great online lingerie stores."

We fired up the PC, considered hundreds of potential ensembles, and rejected them all as too slutty (me) or too tame (her). After a heated battle, we managed to agree on a cute and modestly cut (me) but see-through (her) camisole and panty set.

"I guess it'll do," she relented, handing over her credit card again. "What color are you getting? Say pink and I'm revoking my sponsorship."

"Not pink," I assured her, remembering Danny's response to my borrowed party dress. "Red."

"My little girl's growing up!" she crowed. "Finally!"

The roses arrived the next day, just as I was rushing out for an audition (for an appetite-suppressing herbal supplement—not sure whether I should be flattered or insulted). I opened the door and nearly ran into a deliveryman bearing a huge vase of fresh red blooms. Assuming Jacinda had collected yet another besotted admirer, I blew right past him and was halfway across the courtyard when he yelled after me, "Hey! You Eva Cordes?"

My head whipped around, freeing my feet up to trip over an exposed tree root. "Yeah, that's me," I confirmed, picking myself out of a squat, prickly shrub. "Ow."

"These are for you." He set the roses down on our doorstep and held out his clipboard. "Sign here, please."

I did, after which I dashed back to examine the little white card accompanying the flowers on a clear plastic stick. If

Jacinda had convinced Jeff to up the ante from yesterday's carnations, there was gonna be a hair-pulling, eye-scratching bloodbath . . .

But the roses weren't from Jeff. The card read simply:

> For Eva
> Love, Danny

Love. I clutched the small square of paper in both hands and read it again: *Love, love, love.* Neither of us had used that word before, not seriously anyway.

But there it was, scrawled in blue ink for everyone to see. He loved me.

Or . . . he just felt really, really threatened by Jeff.

When I brought the roses into the apartment, Jacinda looked up from her breakfast of sugar-free Red Bull and a chocolate croissant. "Hey, the Carnation King got his act together, huh?"

"Nope." I flashed the card at her. "Danny."

She scanned the card and started fanning her face with one hand. "Do my eyes deceive me or does that say *'love'*?"

I fixed her with a wintry stare. "It says love."

"So why are you looking at me like that?"

"Because! First of all, Danny can't afford these right now—"

"Whatever." She took a huge bite of croissant. "His dad, like, runs the world at a production studio."

"Yeah, his dad also remarried that hag, Nina Marx, who makes sure that all the money in the family goes to her precious little son. Danny's on a scholarship, hel-lo!"

"Well." She batted her eyelashes. "I guess he's so *in love* that money doesn't matter."

"*Or* he's just saying he is because he's all testosterone-crazed about Jeff."

"A floral pissing contest?" She smirked. "Well, at least he finally got in the game."

"You're so evil."

"Hey, it's not every day that two guys are fighting over you. You should enjoy it while it lasts." She went back to her morning perusal of the G-Spot, *South of Sunset*'s notorious gossip column.

"Jacinda, believe it or not, some of us don't like guys fighting over us—"

"Lie!"

"I don't want all this drama and conflict and . . . and . . . floral pissing contests. I just want Danny."

She threw me a big, open-mouthed wink. "Well, you're gonna get him on Saturday, so what's the big deal?"

"Oh, that reminds me—are you gonna be around this morning to buzz in the FedEx guy with my sexy new undies?"

She shook her head, yawning. "Huh-uh. I have a mani/pedi at ten, and then I have to be in Burbank by noon to do a screen test."

"Damn. Well, where's Coelle?"

"Who knows? Between filming the TV show, pretending to date her fake boyfriend, and losing her shit over the stupid SAT, we probably won't see her again until—wait, here she is!" She jabbed her index finger at a paragraph full of bold names in the G-Spot:

Among the glitterati sharing air kisses and glasses of bubbly after last night's *Buzzkill* premiere: *Twilight's Tempest* doe-eyed ingenue Coelle Banerjee and hot new costar Quentin Palmer. Reps for this toothsome twosome are selling that threadbare "just friends" line, but nobody's buyin'—they arrived together and exchanged some sizzling stares on the red carpet. Will life imitate art? Stay tuned . . .

I scanned the scoop and rolled my eyes. "Hollywood's stupid."

"Don't hate the playa, hate the game," Jacinda trilled. "Speaking of which, you better haul ass if you're gonna make that audition."

So I hauled ass, gritting my teeth as I struggled to maneuver the Goose (which handled like an aircraft carrier) through the heavy morning traffic on Sepulveda Boulevard. When I stopped for a red light, I checked my cell's voicemail, hoping Danny had called. The automated voice announced I had one new message, but it wasn't from Danny:

"Hi, Evie, it's Laurel. I had to call in a few favors and bury a few bodies, but I managed to track down Daphne Farnsworth's private number. I gave her a call and she wants to meet you." (Long pause.) "She's invited you for tea tomorrow at her house in Bel Air. I told her you'd be there." (Another long pause.) "Good luck, pet. You're gonna need it."

7

Even the door knocker was intimidating.
This just seemed like overkill to me. I mean, I'd already had to make it past the ceramic plaques announcing the entrance to Bel Air, the narrow, foliage-lined roads full of hairpin turns, and the staticky intercom mounted by the entrance to a brick-paved driveway—complete with freshly washed Rolls-Royce—to get to the house.

Oh, the house. Let me just say that the Farnsworth estate made Aunt Laurel's posh Bev Hills digs look like a double-wide trailer in Arkansas. This house was straight out of a European history textbook—think Palace of Versailles; the kind of sumptuous spread that could accommodate a temperature-controlled wine cellar, a private screening room, an indoor lap pool, and an underground bowling alley.

Not, of course, that my father's family would ever sully themselves with anything so tacky as bowling. They probably spent their leisure time playing polo and yachting, kicking back with mint juleps, lamenting how hard it was to find good help these days and being all, "I say, old chap . . ."

I shouldn't be so quick to judge. They were, after all, my blood relatives. And they *had* invited me for tea.

But still. I felt a little apprehensive. When I'd called Aunt Laurel back yesterday and asked, "What should I wear?", she'd said, "a bulletproof vest" and laughed in that way that's more grim than amused.

I'd opted for a slightly more subtle outfit—a modest green cashmere sweater and a fluttery J. Mendel skirt I'd borrowed from Coelle. I'd even put on some pearl earrings. How demure.

I'd also hounded Jacinda for finishing school tips—even if she wasn't using them, at least one of us could act like a lady. What was the high society way to hold my knife? Unfold my napkin? Eat cucumber sandwiches with the crusts cut off?

"I got nothing." She'd shrugged when I grilled her. "All I learned in boarding school was how to cheat on finals and get rid of empty vodka bottles without anyone noticing."

So I'd stopped by the bookstore, found a copy of *The Total Moron's Guide to Etiquette,* and crammed on the continental style of dining and how to write the perfect monogrammed thank-you note. Bring on the cucumber sandwiches!

I scrutinized the mansion's ornately carved stone door

frame, but couldn't locate a doorbell. So I took a deep breath, grabbed the heavy brass door knocker, and rapped twice.

Nothing happened.

I couldn't hear anything behind the massive white door, but just as I was about to whip out my cell, call my aunt, and ask her to make sure we'd gotten the time right, the door swung open into a majestic foyer.

A liveried butler ushered me in without a hint of a smile, announced, "Madam will be with you shortly," then took off down the hall. My eyes darted around to the marble pillars, majestic staircase, and, holy crap, was that a real Picasso?

The sharp staccato of high heels on marble echoed around me as Mrs. Daphne Farnsworth approached. I could tell she had been beautiful once, but now she looked skeletal and face-lifted. She was decked out in a tweedy Chanel suit with a string of huge, lustrous gray pearls around her throat. Her silver hair was pulled back in a loose chignon.

I knew I should introduce myself, but I was too terrified to even squeak out a hello.

Her blue eyes glittered as they raked over me; I was acutely aware that my outfit was borrowed, my shoes were cheap, I didn't belong in this lavish, silent world.

"You must be Eva?" She smiled, an effort which seemed to cause her physical pain because it came out more like a grimace.

I nodded wordlessly.

She reached out to take my right hand in both of hers. Her skin felt smooth and cool. I finally started to relax.

"Yes, you're Anatole's daughter. I can see it in the chin and the eyes."

At last! Someone to blame for my gigantic *Precious Moments* eye sockets! But I was glad to know that I looked like him, that people could tell I fit into a family. So I smiled back.

"Will I meet everyone today? The whole family?" I asked, trying not to sound pathetically eager.

Her smile hardened while her eyes gleamed even brighter. "Won't you please wait here for a moment?"

She clicked back down the hall. I watched her go, hoping she was rounding up a passel of sons and daughters and nieces and nephews, all of whom would hopefully be more friendly than she was.

She returned alone a few seconds later, holding a gold-embossed envelope.

"What's this?" I asked, fumbling with the flap.

Her hand closed in a vise grip around my elbow as she steered me toward the front door. "Thank you so much for coming by, Eva."

She was throwing me out? But what about tea? I hadn't even had a chance to show off my continental dining prowess!

"I'm so glad we had this little chat." Her voice was like cold steel.

I ripped open the envelope and found . . . *a check made out to me for $150,000?*

"What is this?" I tried to pull away from her, but she was shockingly strong for someone who looked like she was about to crumble into dust.

"Why, Eva, I'm surprised you have to ask." The smile was still wide under her icy glare. "I'm giving you just what I gave your mother—a nice hefty check to go away and the promise that if you don't, you'll be very sorry indeed."

I thrust the envelope back at her. "But—"

"Now get out. And this time make sure you stay gone."

"Mom?" I yelled into my cellphone, jerking the steering wheel to the left as the Goose fishtailed down the winding roads of Bel Air. "Where are you?"

"Hi, baby girl! What's up?" She sounded breathy and distracted—and sober, for a change—which could mean only one thing: she was with a guy.

"Where are you?"

She feigned confusion. "Right now?"

Definitely with a guy. I just hoped for her sake they weren't in bed, or we were all gonna have a very awkward meet and greet in a few minutes. "Yeah. Right now."

Big sigh. "I'm at the car wash on La Cienega. Why?"

The car wash near the Beverly Center looked unassuming, but it was *the* place to see and be seen. On a busy weekend, you could watch celebrities reading scripts while they waited for their convertibles to be polished to gleaming perfection. "Stay put. I'll be there in fifteen minutes."

"Honey, wait, I'm with Tyson and—"

I hung up and floored it. The Goose shuddered ominously with the sudden infusion of speed, but I was determined to confront her about what Daphne Farnsworth had just said. And if her pathetic excuse for an on-again, off-again boyfriend happened to witness the fireworks, so much the better. He should know what kind of heartless mercenary he was booty calling.

Thanks to a reckless disregard for speed limits, red lights, and bicycle lanes (all that cruising around with Jacinda must have rubbed off on me), I screeched up to the car wash exactly fifteen minutes later.

My mother was perched on one of the outdoor benches plastered with high-end Realtor advertisements. She was doing her best Jackie O impression today—button-down pink suit, bug-eye sunglasses, even dainty white gloves. Except Jackie O never flashed so much cleavage. A bespectacled blond man in a dark suit and tie sat next to her, looking all buttoned-up and sanctimonious. The only way he could have better posture would be if he stapled his spine to a fireplace poker.

"Hey," I said to him as I slammed out of the Goose and tossed my keys to a car wash attendant. "You must be Tyson O'Donnell."

"Marisela?" Tyson turned to my mother for an explanation, but she was distracted by my new ride.

"Oh my God, Evie. What *is* that?"

"That's my car," I announced a tad defensively. "Aunt Laurel bought it for me."

Her coral lips formed a perfect circle as she gaped at the diesel-coughing monstrosity. "And you *took* it? But it's so . . . so . . ."

"I didn't have a whole lot of choice," I fumed. "So unless you're offering to buy me a Maserati . . ."

That shut her up. "Laurel's such a good aunt to you. I don't know what I'd do without her."

"Me, either." I waited patiently while she murmured to

Tyson in low, soothing tones. He walked off toward the register, casting speculative looks my way. When he was out of earshot, I planted a hand on my hip and cocked my head. "So. Mom. Speaking of Aunt Laurel, guess what she did for me? She arranged for me to have lunch with Daphne Farnsworth."

Mom dropped the sleek leather clutch she'd been holding in her right hand. "No!"

"Yes." My gaze never wavered from her face. "And would you like to know what ol' Daph did when I showed up on her doorstep?"

She crouched down to retrieve her purse and avoid my gaze. "She threw you out?"

"Good guess. But before she threw me out, she gave me this." I pulled the check out of my pocket and waved it in her face like a red cape in front of a bull.

Her eyes widened to twice their usual size. "Oh no."

"A hundred and fifty thousand dollars. How much did she give you?"

My mother swallowed hard. "What do you mean?"

"I mean Daphne Farnsworth just gave me one hundred and fifty *thousand* dollars and told me she never wanted to see my face again. So I'm wondering how much she gave you. And what you had to do to get it." I crossed my arms and waited.

Her face turned pink, then gray. "She . . . I . . . what?"

"You heard me. She said I should stay gone *this* time. So why don't you tell me about last time?"

"It's complicated, Eva. You wouldn't understand—" She reached out to me, but I shrunk back.

"I do understand," I corrected. "Finally. Now I know why you dumped me with Grandma and Grandpa. It had nothing to do with wanting to raise me away from the L.A. scene. You'd just rather have cash than your own kid."

Her fist curled around the delicate diamond pendant at her throat. "I know it sounds bad, but you have to believe me—"

The searing afternoon sun, the roar of the car wash, the curious glances we were attracting all receded into the background as we stared each other down.

"I *don't* believe you," I said softly. "You've done nothing but lie since the day I was born. You lie, you cheat, you don't care about anyone but yourself."

"Don't say that. After Anatole died, Daphne found out about you. And she threatened me—she said she would make our lives hell unless—"

I closed my eyes and tried not to yell. "How much did she give you, Mom?"

Big, fat tears started streaking down her cheeks, leaving runny wet trails through her blush and foundation. "She ruined my career! She was going to ruin your whole childhood!"

"*You're* the one who ruined my childhood." I stepped closer, trying to force her to look me in the eye, but she wouldn't. "That's what happened to the other baby, isn't it? Someone waved a fistful of cash and you got rid of my sister or brother?"

She kept sobbing prettily and out of the corner of my eye I saw Tyson approaching.

"Don't do this to me," she begged. "I can't take it."

"You, you, you," I mocked, echoing my aunt's words. She

had tried to warn me about this, the very first day I arrived in California. "It's always about you. I gave up my whole life in Massachusetts and came out here so I could get to know you. And now I do—you're so selfish I can't even look at you." I turned on my heel as Tyson took my mother's hand.

"Is everything all right?" he asked, gruff and bossy. "What's going on?"

"Ask her." I jabbed my thumb toward my mom.

Mom swiped at her eyes with the back of her hand, sniffling as she leaned into him. "This is my daughter, darling, the one I was telling you about."

I laughed caustically. "Don't you mean the *younger sister* you were telling him about?"

She stopped quivering and started screaming. "Would you let that go already? I said I was sorry!"

I simply stared at her for a moment, feet rooted to the asphalt, too full of rage to speak. "I hate you."

"Hey." Tyson gave me a stern, Teddy Roosevelt-esque look. "Don't talk to your mother that way."

I ignored him and headed for the cash register so I could get my so-called car.

"Eva Dominique Cordes, get back here!" Mom hollered. "You can't just leave me like this!"

"Sure I can," I shot back. "Like mother, like daughter."

8

"A hundred and fifty grand?" Jacinda stared at Daphne's check with an expression of abject horror.

"I know." I stretched across the kitchen table, trying to reach the licorice and leftover spaghetti that comprised dinner tonight. (Well, mine and Jacinda's. Coelle had steamed up a vile concoction of broccoli, bok choy, and fresh ginger.) "Pass the Red Vines, por favor."

She handed them over. "What a cheapskate!"

"I know—" I froze, midmunch. "Wait, what?"

"Do you have any idea how much the Farnsworth family is worth?"

I shrugged. "A lot?"

"Hundreds of millions of dollars."

Coelle poured herself another glass of ice water. "That would explain the gigantic compound in Bel Air."

Jacinda waved a piece of licorice around like a professor's pointer. "Yeah, and the beach house in Martha's Vineyard and the ski lodge in Sun Valley and the weekend getaway in Malibu and the penthouse in Manhattan and—"

"They really have all that?" I asked skeptically.

"Hang on, I haven't even mentioned the island retreat in Majorca or the town house in Mayfair. London," she clarified, when I shot her a questioning look. "The Farnsworths make my family look like white trash."

"Oh, I'd say you do a pretty good job of that all by yourself," Coelle muttered through a mouthful of broccoli.

"Shut it, grazer girl."

"And how do you suddenly know all this?" I asked.

She smiled mysteriously. "I have connections."

"So what are you saying?" I put down the licorice as my stomach churned. "I should have held out for my own private island?"

"I'm saying that supercilious hag should've offered you at least half a mil." Jacinda punctuated each word with a whap of her licorice whip. "At *least*. A hundred and fifty thou is an insult."

"Did you guys not hear a word I just said? The 'insult' is kicking me out of the house and practically releasing the hounds on me."

"Did she really have hounds?" Coelle wanted to know. "What kind?"

I looked at her. "Does this sound like a story about dogs to you?"

"I'm just asking," the future veterinarian huffed.

"You should have played hardball," Jacinda repeated. "She would've handed over half a mil without blinking an eye."

"I don't want her money!"

"Don't be stupid; of course you do. If she's gonna call you a money-grubbing gold digger, you might as well get the perks that go with the title."

I gazed down at the bold, flourished signature on the bottom of the check. "Just looking at this makes me want to puke."

"There's an easy cure for that—cash it." Jacinda rubbed her palms together with glee. "Cash it and let's go shopping. Cartier, Van Cleef and Arpels . . . I see diamond necklaces in your immediate future."

"I'm not cashing this!" I dropped the check as if it had burst into flame. "If I cash it, she wins! It means she was right about me!"

"Then what are you going to do with it? Frame it and hang it on the wall with a little plaque that says, 'My family sucks'?" Jacinda shook her head. "I'd rather have jewelry."

"I'm tearing it up," I announced authoritatively. "And then I'm flushing the pieces down the toilet."

"So you're going to let her treat you like crap *and* let her keep her hundred and fifty grand?" Jacinda snorted. "Yeah, that'll show her."

Coelle seemed personally affronted by my plan of action. "You would seriously flush that much money down the toilet?"

"It's blood money!" I shook my fist. "This check cost me my childhood!"

"That check could put me through undergrad at Cornell," she pointed out.

I pushed the check over to her. "Here, take it."

She rolled her eyes. "Don't be melodramatic. I don't need your charity—I have my own trust fund that cost me my own childhood. Besides, don't you need it to put *yourself* through college?"

I didn't answer because this question raised a lot of issues I wasn't prepared to deal with. Like where I was going to college. And when. And what I was going to do with the rest of my life now that the big mother-daughter reunion had crashed and burned.

So I just blustered on with, "Anything I buy with this money will be tainted."

"Then take your diamond necklace to one of those crazy psychic healers on Sunset and have the aura cleansed," Jacinda instructed. "Now grab your purse and let's go. First stop, the bank, next stop, Rodeo Drive. Ooh, you know where we should go? Neil Lane. They have the best estate jewelry—"

"Jacinda. Open your ears. I'm not cashing this check."

"Then who will I shop with?" she whined. "I'm so sick of being friends with paupers."

"Then go hang out with all your Richie Rich friends from boarding school," Coelle said.

"I can't." She shook out her long blonde hair, suddenly transfixed by the view outside the kitchen window. "There

88   BETH KILLIAN

was a slight misunderstanding with one of their ex-boyfriends and they *totally* overreacted and now . . ."

"Someday someone is going to steal your boyfriend and you're going to find out how it feels," Coelle warned.

"Who?" Jacinda scoffed. "Who in the three-one-oh is better at man wrangling than I am? Anyway, you don't even have a real boyfriend, so I don't want to hear it from you."

Coelle grinned. "Breaking news: Quentin might be my real boyfriend."

I stopped scowling down at my check and gaped at her. "Really?"

"What?" Jacinda seemed even more shocked than me. "When? Where? How?"

She nibbled her bok choy and played coy. "After I started dancing with him last night we got to talking and . . . well, I'm scheduled to go to a press event with him on Saturday, but he asked if I wanted to get together before then. Just the two of us—no cameras, no reporters, no PR spin. I'm going to his place tomorrow night."

"Well, say hi to Jeff." I shook my head. "And tell him to cease and desist with the flowers."

"Yeah, I saw the roses when I got back from the set." She nodded in the direction of the huge arrangement of red blooms. "Classy."

"Oh, those are from Danny," I corrected.

"Macho display of resources?" She considered this for a moment. "Better late than never, I guess."

"Why does everybody keep saying that?" I asked.

"Anyway, on Saturday, Quentin and I are supposed to go

to this fund-raiser for an animal rescue group in Orange County. I had my publicist set it up. She said it's important to choose a cause, and that's mine. So if you guys want to come . . ."

"Can't." Jacinda didn't offer any more details. Very unusual for her.

I shook my head. "Me, either."

"Yeah, she's got big plans for Saturday: lose virginity," Jacinda supplied. "Talk about better late than never."

"Oh, good for you!" Coelle patted my hand.

"Could you guys be any more condescending?" I gnawed on my licorice. "God. When are you going to stop treating me like a FOB?" (FOB = "fresh off the boat," aka the naïve blondes flying into LAX every day with dreams of instant stardom who couldn't find their way from the 310 to the 818 with a Thomas Guide, a dashboard GPS system, and a gun to their heads.)

"I'll stop treating you like a FOB when you stop acting like a FOB," Jacinda declared. "Hey, did your undies come yet?"

"Dunno—I've been too busy disowning my mother and deciding how to spend my bastard legacy to worry about FedEx."

Coelle pointed wordlessly toward the hall table by the front door, where a small cardboard box rested against the wall.

"Open it! Open it!" Jacinda's enthusiasm was contagious, and I grabbed a paring knife and attacked the box. Two minutes later, we were all oohing and ahhing over a lace-trimmed, transparent red camisole set.

"Try it on!" Jacinda urged.

I blinked. "For you? I don't think so."

"Oh, come on!"

"You might as well," Coelle chimed in. "We can make sure that shade of red is right for your skin tone. Reds can be tricky. Just try on the top."

And that is why, when the doorbell rang and Jacinda flung it open without even bothering to glance through the peep-hole and my aunt Laurel walked in, I was wearing a slutty lin-gerie top with my jeans and boots.

My skin felt hot and prickly as I hugged my arms over my chest to shield my nipples from her apprising glance.

"Nice shirt." She didn't even bat an eye. "Did you borrow that from your mother?"

"I can explain," I sputtered, since neither of my room-mates uttered a peep.

"Don't," she advised, a hint of a smile playing at the cor-ners of her mouth. "All I ask is that you not wear that on au-ditions. It might send the wrong message about the agency."

"No, I would never," I assured her. "I was just . . . we were trying . . . it's Jacinda's fault."

"Isn't it always?" Her smile disappeared as she surveyed the designer-label wreckage strewn over the floor. "I like what you girls have done with the place."

Coelle scooped up an armful of clothes from the patch of carpet directly in front of her. "It's not usually like this," she lied. "We take very good care of this apartment because, you know, we're so grateful to Allora."

"Totally." Jacinda put on her most wide-eyed, innocent expression. "We were just sorting through all our old stuff to, uh, make a donation to Goodwill."

I yanked my sweater back over my head and did my best impression of a mentally healthy, well-adjusted teenager.

"Listen, girls, do you think I could have a moment alone with Eva?"

"Absolutely!" My roommates raced upstairs, tripping over each other in their haste to get out of firing range.

Laurel looked at me. I looked at her.

"You'll never guess who just called me at work," she started.

"Is this about the thing at the car wash?" I asked wearily.

"Yes, this is about the thing at the car wash. Marisela says you started a screaming match in front of the lunchtime Lexus crowd?"

"*She* started the screaming match. You know how she is."

"Indeed I do. And I'm not here to talk about the screaming match, per se. I'm here to discuss the inciting incident of the screaming match."

I narrowed my eyes. "Have you spent all afternoon arguing with contract lawyers again?"

"Maybe. Where's the check?"

I jerked my head toward the kitchen table.

She strode over in her sensible black pumps and examined the figures inked after "Pay to the order of Eva Cordes."

"God, what a bitch," she muttered under her breath.

"You were right," I admitted grudgingly. "Again. Happy?"

"Oh, Evie." She nibbled her bottom lip. "You want to talk about this? Feelings and all that?"

"No, I'm good, thanks." I had to laugh at her expression of relief.

"So what are you going to do with the money?" she asked.

"Put it through a shredder."

"Oh no you're not."

"Oh yes I am." I tried to reclaim the check, but she stuffed it into her briefcase. "Fine. If I can't shred it, I'll donate it all to charity."

"Wrong again."

"Says who?"

"Says the woman who built her own agency from the ground up with the sweat of her brow and no one to stake her a big chunk of capital. You are not going to throw this money away just because you're having a fit of pique."

"I am so!" I debated wrestling the briefcase out of her hand.

"Listen, pet. It's tough out there. You think you're always going to have a cushy apartment and commercial residuals and nothing to do but party and gossip and date? Once you get out of college, you'll find out—real life sucks. You're going to need food, shelter, car insurance. And don't even get me started on real estate prices out here. Only an idiot would walk away from this money."

"It's my choice," I insisted.

"No, it's not. You're living in *my* apartment building, working for *my* agency, and you're going to sign this check over to me and let me invest it for you until the day you need it. Because, trust me, that day will come."

"Why don't you just invest it for Mom? She's the one who'll do anything for a buck."

Laurel froze, midlecture. "What do you mean?"

"Daphne told me that's how she got Mom to ship me off to Massachusetts. A big, fat check to pack me up and pretend the whole thing never happened. Nice."

My aunt didn't say a word, but I knew what she was thinking from her panicked expression.

"And yeah, I know what happened to the other baby. She did one of her faux nervous breakdowns the minute I brought it up, but I don't feel sorry for her after what she did."

She inhaled sharply. "She told you about Thomas?"

I blinked. "Who's Thomas?"

She blinked back. "What are you talking about?"

"What are *you* talking about?"

"Nothing, " she said, way too quickly.

Thomas? What the hell? The Farnsworths didn't have a son named Thomas. And unless my mom had named her fetus before she aborted it, which was pushing the sick-and-twisted envelope even for her . . .

I kept my next question light and casual. "Mom *did* have an abortion, didn't she?"

"Well, that's what she told you, right?" Aunt Laurel shrugged. "So that's what happened."

Now that I thought about it, Mom hadn't really denied or confirmed anything. She'd just cried pathetically. And when Aunt Laurel fell back on the dodgy, answer-a-question-with-a-question routine, that could only mean one thing: lies, lies, and more lies.

"Who's Thomas?" I repeated.

"No one! Nothing! It's none of your business!"

"Don't make me break into your study again!"

"Try it," she dared. "I moved all my files to the agency safe. I'd love to see you get past Harper and a state-of-the-art security system."

Damn. "So you admit you have something to hide?"

"I admit nothing! You're the one with the breaking-and-entering tendencies; I don't have to justify myself to you!"

"Fine," I said. "I'll go to the press. I'll score a sit-down on *Access Hollywood* and appeal to viewers all over the country to help me find my long-lost brother, Thomas."

"I'll call *Access Hollywood* before you go on and tell them they'll never get another Allora client interview if they sit down with you," she shot back.

"Why? Why are you always torturing me?" I keened.

"Because I love you," she snarled.

"Well, stop!"

"I'm trying, believe me!"

"Give me my money!" I held out my hand.

"No way in hell." She whipped a gold pen out of her briefcase, along with the controversial check. "You are going to sign this over to me, missy, and I am going to make you rich whether you like it or not." She forced my fingers around the pen and yanked me over to the kitchen counter. "One day you'll thank me for this."

9

"Wow," I said when I arrived at Quentin's condo for a big heart-to-heart with Jeff. "Nice digs."

"No kidding." Jeff grinned. "This place beats the hell out of a hotel. We've got GameCube, PlayStation, Xbox, a plasma TV, and enough processed meat products to last us till spring."

"And a balcony," I added, peering over his shoulder into the white-carpeted, pizza box-strewn living room.

"Oh yeah, that, too," he agreed, looking longingly at the gaming system hooked up to the huge television.

"Hey." I snapped my fingers in his face to break his reverie. "Do you want to talk about what's going on with us or do you want to play Grand Theft Auto?"

"Can't we talk *while* we play Grand Theft Auto?"

I just looked at him.

"Fine. If we have to be all serious, we'd better go down to the pool." He glanced back into the apartment. "Quentin's still in bed and I think he has a girl over."

Ooh! Maybe it was Coelle. But Coelle had an early call time today. . . . Ooh! Maybe she finished filming early and came right over to get a little noontime pick-me-up.

"You're getting the full frat house experience and you're not even in college yet," I congratulated him.

"I know." His grin widened. "College is gonna rock."

"Yeah. Speaking of college." I cleared my throat as he stepped into the hall and closed the door behind him. "You're off to Dartmouth in September, right?"

"Uh-huh." He shoved his hands into the pockets of his baggy khaki pants as we strolled toward the elevators. "So?"

"So did you plan on us doing the long-distance relationship thing?" I asked. "For four years?"

He shrugged. "I don't know."

" 'Cause I don't think I'm moving back to Massachusetts."

He looked up. "What about Leighton?"

"I might apply to schools out here instead. UCLA, maybe USC, Pomona . . ."

"You just want to go to UCLA because Danny goes there," he accused.

"Not really."

"Yes, really! Come on, Eva. Don't be one of those girls who schedules her whole life around her boyfriend. You hate those girls."

"I'm not one of those girls," I argued. "You're just mad because I'm not going to follow *you* around."

He didn't say anything.

"What the hell's going on? Seriously? You show up here, out of the blue, and decide you're in love with me? Just like that? And oh, by the way, here's an *engagement ring*?"

"You don't have to sound so horrified," he muttered.

"Well, what did you think I would say?"

Another shrug. "I don't know."

The elevator doors dinged open and we stepped inside. "No, for real. What would you have done if I had said yes, let's get married?"

"Well . . . I hadn't really planned that part out," he admitted. "But I thought, you know, if I could get your attention . . ."

"Believe me, you have my attention. Mine *and* Danny's."

He sneered when I mentioned Danny. "You hooked up with him in a hurry."

"I guess, but even if there were no Danny, we"—I waved my index finger between him and me—"would never work."

"Sure we would!"

"No, we wouldn't." As we arrived on the ground floor and stepped into the building's lobby, I managed to look at everything but him. "I mean, I do love you, but not that way."

"If you say I'm like your brother again . . ."

"Well, you are! I can't help it! We ate paste together and built tree forts! I used to stuff Kleenex in your nose after Tyler Wall beat you up every day in sixth grade!"

He stiffened as we pushed through the glass doors to a sparkling blue swimming pool surrounded by white slatted chairs. "So you're saying you'd be interested if I weren't such a wuss."

"No! I'm just saying . . . sometimes it's better to just be friends. Especially us. We're great as friends. The best!"

"I know. So why couldn't we be great as more than friends?" he pressed.

I collapsed into one of the chairs shaded by a potted palm tree and gave up on logic. "When did you suddenly decide you like me as more than a friend?"

"It was a gradual thing, I guess. It's not like I woke up one day and—"

"Was it when I hooked up with Bryan Dufort?"

He shrugged.

"Was it when I left for California?" I paused. "You only want me when someone else does."

"No!"

"Yes! You knew I liked Bryan, so *bam,* you asked me to homecoming! You knew I was dating Danny out here, so *bam,* you show up with a ring."

"That's not true!" His ears were turning red again. "I was interested way before Bryan Dufort."

"Then why didn't you ever say anything?"

"I don't—"

I held up a hand. "I've had it with the 'I don't knows'! You only want me when I'm not all about you. Or is that just an amazing coincidence?"

"You're saying you never had a crush on me?" He sounded incredulous. "You never once wondered what it'd be like if we . . . ?"

I flinched. "Not really. There's no chemistry."

He leaned forward. "We could have chemistry."

I shook my head sadly. "I don't think so."

That's when he kissed me. Right on the lips.

He was completely into it, eyes closed, forehead furrowed with intensity. And I . . . well, I didn't actually have a brother, but if I did, and if I kissed him on the mouth (I know, *eww*), I imagined it would feel pretty much like this.

I stared at the pores on the bridge of his nose until he realized that I wasn't kissing him back. When he opened his eyes and pulled away, I tried to be nice. "Sorry," I said. "It's just . . . I have a boyfriend."

"You didn't feel *anything*?" He sounded incredulous.

"I have a boyfriend," I repeated, because I didn't want to hurt his feelings.

His whole face went as red as his ears. I couldn't tell if he was mad or mortified. "Then at least take the ring."

"No!"

"Just hang on to it for a while." He slapped the black velvet box into my palm and closed my fingers around it. "See how you feel next week. Maybe you'll change your mind."

I thrust the box back at him. "I'm not going to change my mind."

"You might." He gave it back to me.

"I won't." I tried to toss the box back to him but missed—

kerplunk, it splashed into the pool. There's a reason I was always chosen last for volleyball team in gym class.

"Great." He peered down into the deep end. "Now I can't return it to the jewelry store. Do you know how much that thing cost?"

As I got up from my deck chair to assess the damage, a flash of blonde and blue caught my eye. I turned toward the glass doors that led to the lobby and I saw her.

Jacinda Crane-Laird. Sporting a full-on bed head of unconditioned hair, black sunglasses that covered half her face, and a dark blue man's shirt that hung almost to her knees.

"Oh my God." I grabbed Jeff's arm and pointed. "What is she doing here?"

I didn't wait for his response. "Hey!" I charged into the lobby as she was exiting onto the sidewalk. *"Hey!"*

"What?" She whipped around, her expression guilty behind her shades. "Oh, it's you. What are you doing here?"

"What are *you* doing here?" I countered.

"I asked you first."

I narrowed my eyes. "Why do you look like a hangover on heels?"

She shoved the sunglasses up on top of her head and squinted at me with bloodshot eyes. "Because I'm hungover, bitch."

"Are you . . . ?" Suspicion swirled through my brain. "Tell me you're not doing what I think you're doing."

She tried to look innocent. "Okay. I'm not doing what you think I'm doing. Happy?"

"You're sleeping with Quentin! No wonder you wouldn't answer when I knocked on your door this morning."

"Wow, you're good." She unwrapped a piece of gum and popped it into her mouth. "You sure you're not secretly CIA?"

I curled my upper lip in disgust. "Poaching your own roommate's man? That is a new low, even for you."

"I didn't know, okay?" She looked embarrassed for the first time since I'd met her. "I didn't know that Coelle actually liked him until yesterday. She never likes anyone! They were supposed to just be photo-op dating!"

Jeff had followed me out to the street, but I waved him away with both hands. "So?"

"So I had already had my way with him by then! Twice! She said she didn't give a rat's ass about him. She said she didn't have time to date. This isn't my fault."

My eyebrows shot up. "And the sleeping over at his condo and coming down at noon looking like a hot mess in his shirt?"

"Okay, that part might be a little bit my fault," she conceded. "I came over last night to tell him we had to break up, and things got a little out of hand. Listen, don't tell Coelle, okay?"

"Jacinda!"

She tried to toss her hair, but her signature move didn't work so well when she hadn't used a comb or conditioner. "Keep your mouth shut. I'm serious."

"Well, what are you going to do when she finds out?"

"She's never going to find out because we're never going to tell her."

"What if Quentin tells her?"

"Him?" she scoffed. "Please. He's a soulless pretty boy. Coelle can have him. He's kind of underwhelming in bed, if you know what I mean." She dropped her sunglasses back over her eyes with a smirk. "But I guess you *don't* know. See ya, Snow White."

"Who's Snow White?" Jeff looked mystified as Jacinda sauntered off toward the parking garage.

"Not me," I assured him. Not after this weekend, anyway.

10

The valets at the Somerset Hotel didn't smirk or snicker when I pulled up in the Goose. They acted as though I had presented them with a brand-new Maybach, helping me lift my overnight bag out of the backseat and calling me "miss." My anticipation built as I walked under a vine-covered wooden overhang into a lobby done up in dark wood and polished brass. The uniformed desk clerk glanced over with a polite smile. "Welcome to the Somerset. May I help you?"

I put on a posh, slightly bored voice and headed toward the counter. "I should have an oceanfront suite reserved for tonight. The last name is Cordes, C-O-R-D-E-S."

She typed this into her computer and nodded. "You're all set, miss. Your traveling companion has already checked in."

"He has?" I was suddenly very aware of the elasticized pressure of the red panties on my hips under my skirt. "Great."

She tapped at her keyboard and handed me a small plastic key card. "You're in room three-twenty-eight. Just go down that hall to the elevator banks and up to the third floor. Please let our staff know if there's anything we can do to make your stay here more enjoyable."

If all went according to plan, the hotel staff wouldn't be seeing or hearing from either of us until checkout time tomorrow. I had everything we needed to make our stay enjoyable right in my suitcase.

The ride up to the third floor was excruciatingly slow, and my stomach felt like it was doing backflips. When the doors finally opened, I hurried down the corridor until I spied the oval brass wall plaque engraved with 328, then took a moment to square my shoulders, smooth my hair, pop a breath mint, and take a few calming breaths.

The door swung inward while I was still getting up the nerve to knock. "Eva?"

In his khakis, black sweater, and UCLA baseball cap, Danny looked so reassuringly normal that I laughed with relief. "How did you know I was out here?"

"I didn't." He lifted the silver bucket in his right hand and leaned over to give me a kiss. "I was going to get ice for the champagne."

"Ooh, you brought champagne?" I breezed past him to check out the room.

"Well, you booked the hotel and went lingerie shopping—I thought I should contribute *something*." He took the bulky black bag out of my hand and placed it on a white-upholstered bench at the foot of the bed.

"Wow. I have good taste," I congratulated myself, surveying the massive bed, the mossy green velvet sofa, and the blue ocean glittering beyond the plantation shutters. This suite radiated intimacy and harmony—just what we needed to get past the whole mess with Jeff. "So listen. About that card that came with roses . . ."

"Oh, that." He put down the ice bucket and shifted his weight from one foot to the other. "I just wanted you to know."

"Know what?" I pressed. I knew I shouldn't torture him like this, but a girl wants to hear these things before she whips off her clothes, right? Besides, he was cute when he got all disconcerted and inarticulate.

He looked like he was in physical pain. "To know that I, you know. Love you."

I grabbed his hand and tugged him toward the balcony. "Come on, let's watch the sun set."

He followed me out into the damp breeze. "That's *it*?"

I wrapped my arms around his waist and squeezed. "You were expecting something more?"

"Yeah." He squeezed back a little harder.

"Like what?" I pretended to be clueless. "Like 'I love you, too'?"

"Don't hurt yourself."

I crooked my index finger. "C'mere, then. I have something to say to you."

He scowled. "I'm not sure I want to hear it anymore."

"Yes, you do." I went up on tiptoe. "Come closer."

When he leaned in, I asked, in the sexiest whisper I could manage, "Are you going to take off the baseball cap when we get down and dirty?"

"I'll take it off right now." He grabbed me, threw me over his shoulder, and carried me back into the bedroom.

"Wait!" I squealed as he tossed me onto the fluffy down comforter. "What about the sunset?"

"Screw the sunset."

"Mmm." I stopped squirming when he kissed me. "You may have a point there."

We kissed and kissed and pretty soon, things started coming off. My sandals. His shoes. The infamous baseball cap.

His shirt.

My dress.

At that point, things got ever so slightly dicey. Once I helped him pull the black silk over my head, I felt so *naked.* I mean, I know that was the whole point—I had suffered through a Brazilian wax for this very reason—but once it was just me and him and the see-through red camisole and panties . . .

"You are gorgeous," he murmured, staring down at me.

I crossed my arms awkwardly over my stomach. "Thanks. You said red was your favorite color, so . . ."

"See-through is my favorite color," he corrected, moving my wrists so he could kiss the patch of stomach just above my navel.

Relax, I told myself. Calm down. Breathe in, breath out . . .

The navel kissing ceased. "Eva?"

I opened one eye and looked at him. "Yeah?"

"You okay?"

"Of course." But my giggle sounded nervous, even to me. "I'm just in the throes of passion."

"Really. Because you look like you're trying to prepare yourself for a prison camp interrogation."

I propped myself up on my elbows and gave him a long, sloppy kiss. "I'm having the best time ever."

"Me, too." He started to undo his belt buckle.

I rocketed into a sitting position, practically knocking him unconscious as my head thunked into his. "I have to, um . . . hang on a second. Wait right here."

"I'm not going anywhere," he assured me, rubbing the burgeoning bump on his forehead.

I skittered into the hotel room's huge, green-tiled bathroom, turned on the faucet full blast, and gave myself a serious talking-to in the mirror. *What the hell is wrong with you?* I demanded of my reflection. *You're finally going to do it! You have a romantic hotel room, a fresh bikini wax, and a great guy who's probably going to be a major league baseball pitcher! Who loves you! What else could you possibly ask for?*

Nothing. That was the answer to that question. I was never going to get a better opportunity than this.

"Grow up," I admonished myself. "And put some more lipstick on."

But my lipstick was still in my purse out in the bedroom, so I had to settle for pinching my cheeks, hitching up my camisole straps, and marching back out to seduce Danny Bristow.

"I'm back," I announced, edging onto the mattress. "Did you miss me?"

He looked confused. "Are you okay?"

I covered his mouth with my hand. "Shut up and kiss me."

He did. And it was great.

Until the tip of his thumb eased under the edge of my panties.

Take two of lunging upward and nearly giving him a concussion.

"Sorry," I wailed, collapsing back against the pillows. *"Sorry."*

He rolled over to one side of the bed. "What's going on, Eva? Tell me before I get permanent brain damage."

"Ouch." I glanced at the red swelling near his temple. "I know, my skull's like titanium."

"Do you not want to do this?" He sounded both hurt and frustrated, and I scooted over to rest my head on his shoulder.

"I definitely want to do this," I assured him.

"Then what is going on?"

"Nothing!" I protested, desperate to convince him. "I just—"

"Is this about Jeff?" he demanded.

"What? No! Why does everything keep coming back to Jeff?"

"You tell me!" He got up and stalked across the room, looking like a Calvin Klein model with an attitude problem.

I stretched out my arms toward him. "Danny, come on. How could you even—"

"Everything was fine with us until he showed up." He

grabbed his sweater off the carpet and yanked it over his head.

"What are you doing?" I cried. "Don't put your clothes *on*!"

"Too late." He sat down on the white bench and crammed his foot into a sock.

I knelt on the comforter, watching him seethe under the misapprehension that Jeff was the reason I was so nervous, and realized I had no choice but to tell him the truth.

"Okay." I let out a huge, pent-up breath. "I admit it: I'm being a freak. And I'm sorry. But this has nothing to do with Jeff."

He glanced at me, but didn't say a word.

I drew my knees up to my chest and rested my chin on them. "I *so* did not want to get into this tonight, but here's the thing." I paused, cringing in anticipation of the embarrassment to come.

"What's the thing?" he prompted.

"The thing is, it's kind of my first time."

He froze, his foot halfway into a shoe.

"And the last guy I made out with in high school, he was drunk and I was drunk and there was some, like, out-of-control groping, so I guess I'm a little gun-shy—"

His expression had gone from accusatory to horrified. "And you're just telling me all this *now*?"

I nodded. "I didn't want it to get in the way. But obviously, it's too late for that."

"Why didn't you—" He broke off, his eyebrows snapping

together. "Hang on. Was the drunk guy's name Bryan Du-fort?"

"Yeah. How did you know?"

"Because Jeff mentioned him the day he showed up at your doorstep with an engagement ring."

"So? Who cares?"

"I do!" He began collecting the rest of his stuff strewn around the room. "I can't believe you told Jeff about this and not me."

"Come on," I cajoled. "Don't get mad. It happened when I was back in Massachusetts; I hadn't even met you yet. Besides, Jeff and I talk about *everything*."

As soon as the words were out of my mouth, I knew I'd made a major mistake.

He slammed open the closet and lifted out a tan over-night bag.

I gasped. "Where are you going?"

"I'm leaving." His voice was flat but furious.

"I can't believe this!" I pulled the comforter up around me like a cape. "Just because I don't mention every little detail of my entire life—"

"Like the fact that you're a virgin?"

Somehow this sounded even worse coming from him than from Jacinda.

"Can we please just forget I ever said anything?" I begged.

"I'm out of here. Why don't you call your future husband, Jeff? I'm sure he'd be happy to trot on over and *talk*."

"Jeff has nothing to do with this!"

He shoved his wallet back into his pocket. "I'm not going to hang around waiting for you to decide whether you want him or me."

"Hel-lo! I'm lying here, throwing myself at you, and you can't figure out who I want?"

He headed for the door. "It doesn't matter anymore who you want."

"You're seriously leaving?"

"Yep."

"But you . . . don't you want me?"

"Not anymore."

Any other guy—a *normal* guy—would be too clouded by hormones and lust to think clearly by now. A normal guy would just succumb to temptation. But not Danny. "My roommates are right—you *are* thirty-five!" I cried, stung by his rejection. "You're just a . . . a balding, suburban accountant trapped in a baseball player's body! Those washboard abs are false advertising!"

He walked out on me without a single look back, leaving me alone with the sunset and the champagne and the big, empty bed.

By the time I got home, the sky had turned gray and cloudy. A light drizzle dotted the Goose's windshield. I slung my purse over my shoulder and dragged my suitcase behind me as I headed toward the apartment. The outdoor light by the mailboxes had burned out, so I didn't see Bissy Billington until I was practically stepping on her little white boots.

"Well, well, well. If it isn't Eva Cordes, world-famous booty shaker," she purred. "Fancy meetin' you here."

I kept my head down and tried to push past her, but there was someone else blocking my path. In the darkening shadows, I couldn't make out a face, but then I saw it. The flash of a gold tooth in the moonlight.

"Hey, shorty," said a gruff, yet oddly high-pitched voice.

"Oh, please God, no." I dropped my head in despair.

"Hells yeah!" Caleb "C Money" Marx stepped forward, resplendent in a puffy black leather coat and matching leather Soji hat. "Why you never call me back? I picked out a sickish ringtone for your sweet ass!"

If I were a superhero, C Money would be my Lex Luthor. A freakish mix of Clay Aiken and Vanilla Ice who fancied himself the next Jay-Z, he was Danny's stepbrother and the bane of my existence. Aunt Laurel had forced me to go on a date with him last month, which had led to meeting Danny, which had led to our top-secret relationship, which had ended with Danny storming out of the hotel room tonight.

"I'm in no mood for this," I warned.

"Why not?" Bissy slipped her arm through C Money's. "Afraid you're going to figure out what you're missing?"

My mouth dropped open. "Are you two *together*?"

"Bingo." She laughed shrilly, her sleek blonde ponytail swishing against the diamond stud in his ear.

"Yeah, we crispin'," he agreed.

"Well . . ." I shrugged. "Good luck with that."

C Money looked Bissy over approvingly, then sidled up to me and whispered, "She's one phat bunny, but baby, you mac-a-licious. So if you ever wanna get back with your b-boy . . ."

I shoved him away.

"Why you skitzing, girl? And what's up with that raggedy hooptie?" He regarded the Goose with scorn. "Guess you don't need no ice and no billie."

"Whatever," I muttered. "Leave me alone."

He looked disappointed. "That's all you got to say?"

"Stop shoving your fake relationship in my face and move it," I warned.

"Hey!" His nostrils flared. "We ain't flamboasting!"

"Yeah." Bissy stamped her foot. "We are *in love*!"

I rolled my eyes and searched for terminology that he would understand. "Will you please quit . . . faking jacks, homes?"

"Forget her, Caleb—she missed her chance. She's still throwing herself at Danny." Bissy's eyes gleamed. "I saw them kissing a few days ago."

"You still rolling with that feeble wank?" He shook his scrawny fist. "I'm telling my mom! I'm telling your aunt!"

"You got a problem?" I put up my dukes. "Don't bring it to your momma. Let's go, G."

He backed up. "I don't fight no girl."

"Scared I'll kick your ass?" I broke out a few of the moves I'd learned in the Capoeira class Coelle had dragged me to last week. "Bring it. Take your best shot."

"C'mon, boo, hop on the side." He yanked Bissy toward his Hummer. She stumbled after him, casting desperate looks over her shoulder to see if her pathetic attempt to make me jealous had worked.

When I headed into the courtyard, I caught Mrs. Billington watching me from the kitchen window of their apartment.

I considered giving her the finger, then decided it wasn't worth the lecture I'd get from my aunt. So I just hurried toward my apartment and promised myself a reward for surviving this hellish night. As I twisted my key in the lock, I heard a footstep behind me.

"Hey." Jeff's voice made me drop my bags and clutch at my heart. "You're back."

"Oh my God, what are you doing?" Heart hammering, I leaned over to retrieve my luggage. "You scared the crap out of me."

"Sorry." His bushy blond hair had gotten even bushier from the rain. "I was waiting for you, and nobody's home."

"Of course nobody's home—it's Saturday night." Coelle was probably off with her new boyfriend and Jacinda . . . well, actually, maybe Jacinda was off with Coelle's new boyfriend.

"You're home," he pointed out. "Guess I'm lucky you didn't have any big date plans."

I slumped against the door frame. "What do you want, Jeff?"

"What happened to you?" he asked. "Were you crying?"

"No," I lied, trying to keep my voice steady.

"Yeah, you were," he decided. "What's up? Problems with Danny?"

I threw up my hands. "Do you guys have, like, secret man-problem radar detectors that you're not telling me about?"

"He doesn't appreciate you," Jeff informed me. "He doesn't understand you the way I do."

"No one understands me the way you do," I pointed out. "My grandma had to shave the back of my head because you tied me to a pine tree full of sap. It's hard to compete with that, and I'm not sure I want anyone to try."

"I get it." He looked so calm and familiar. "You want me to back off. I get it. And I will."

"You will?"

"Yeah. If you really want this other guy, I'll back off." He shrugged. "But seriously, how great can he be if he makes you look so sad and disappointed?"

I considered this for a moment. And then another moment. And then I opened my mouth to ask what I knew was a dangerous question:

"Want to come in?"

11

"So what happened with Danny?" Jeff asked as he reached across the table for a slice of the greasy pizza we'd ordered. "You guys have a fight?"

"I really don't want to talk about him," I said. "Let's talk about something else. *Anything* else."

Jeff brightened. "But it's not working out? You think you might break up?"

"What did I just say?"

"God. Ever since you got famous, you are so freaking touchy."

"I've done one national commercial. I'd hardly call that famous."

"One national commercial that aired during the Super Bowl," he pointed out.

I picked the olives (his idea) off my pizza. "Please. I'm nobody without my aunt's connections. Now Jacinda and Coelle—*they're* famous."

"But you're out here making your way, doing your thing."

I laughed dryly. "And everything is working out so well."

"It is!" he insisted. "You have new friends, a real apartment, guys beating down your door . . ."

"A dead father, a lunatic mother, and a mysterious sibling who may or may not exist," I finished. "Yeah. It's a fairy tale come true."

He paused for a sip of Coke before stammering, "You don't need me anymore."

"Of course I do." It felt so comforting to let my guard down and talk to him the way I used to. "You're my best friend. Just because I moved to Los Angeles doesn't mean I'm going to forget you."

"I guess." He looked supremely uncomfortable. "But when you left, I missed my window to take it to the next level. You were gone and I was still stuck suffering through Spanish class and watching the idiot crew jocks get wasted at keggers and waiting for college to start so I could sign up for four more years of the same pseudo-academic bullshit."

"A midsenior-year crisis?" I nodded. "Had one of those myself, and *voila,* here I am."

He stared at the pizza box. "I wanted to give it one more shot with you."

"Yeah, but you're freaking me out, because it's like I don't even recognize you anymore. What happened to the real Jeff Oerte? The one who used to force me to stay up all night watching those crazy John Woo movies—"

"*Hardboiled*—best movie ever made," he interjected.

"—and making fun of *Hamlet* and stuff?"

" 'Oh, pernicious woman!' "

"Exactly. What happened to that guy? I miss him." I braced my knees against the tabletop, leaning back against the top of the chair.

"I'm still that guy." He looked defeated. "The same nice, boring, brother guy. That's all I'll ever be to you."

"Look," I said softly. "I want us to be friends forever. I want us to keep in touch through college and go to each other's weddings and send Christmas presents to each other's kids someday. I don't have a lot of family. I need to hang on to the people I love. And if we cross that line . . ."

"It'll ruin the friendship. Blah, blah, blah. All those stupid clichés." He sighed. "I can't compete with Mr. All-Star Baseball Player. I know I have no chance—Jacinda already told me you're sleeping with him. So if he makes you happy . . ."

I sniffled.

"Hey." He got up from his chair and circled the table to crouch down next to me. "Seriously. What is going on with you?"

"PMS?" I tried hopefully.

"No way. If you had PMS, you'd be carving me up with a steak knife, not sitting there with a sad little Yoda face." He put an arm around my shoulder. "Did something happen with Mr. All-Star?"

I nodded.

"Something I'm going to have to kick his ass for?"

I smiled in the midst of my emotional breakdown. "Just like you kicked Bryan Dufort's?"

"I'll get around to that," he blustered. "There's still a few months left before graduation. When he least expects it, there's going to be a reckoning—it's going to be like that scene in *Hardboiled* where they're in the hospital and—"

"I remember, I remember." I wiped my eyes with the back of my hand.

"So what'd Mr. Perfect do?"

"Well. You know how Jacinda told you I was having sex with him?"

He flinched. "Yeah."

"That was a lie."

"Really?"

"Sort of. I planned to have sex with him, I wanted to have sex with him, but he . . ." My whole face crumpled up as I made squeaky noises of despair. "He didn't want me."

"He didn't?" Jeff could not have looked more flummoxed if I had smacked him in the head with a two-by-four.

But I couldn't say anything more—the rejection and the humiliation were too raw.

"Well, that guy's an idiot," Jeff declared.

"No, he's right," I managed to say between shuddery breaths. "It's me. I'm too . . . I'm not . . . I'm just . . ."

"Hey." Jeff pushed my hair back from my face. "You're beautiful, you're smart, you're sexy . . ."

"Then why doesn't he see that?" I sobbed. "Why did he just walk out and leave me?"

"He doesn't deserve you."

"But—"

"Hey." He squeezed my shoulder. "He doesn't appreciate what he has. I would never do that to you."

Our eyes met, and he leaned forward to kiss me. I met him halfway.

I didn't feel any of the tingly chemistry I had with Danny, but this time, kissing Jeff felt nice. Warm. Safe. I closed my eyes and tried to block out all the anguish of the last few hours. Going numb would be such a relief. And Jeff and I made perfect sense: we'd loved each other platonically for years, I was already wearing my see-through lingerie, and I had a pack of condoms in my purse. All things considered, I was as ready as I'd ever be.

Besides. Unlike some people I could mention, Jeff actually *wanted* me. He'd flown three thousand miles to prove it.

I took his hand and tried to smile as I led him up the stairs to my bedroom.

"Oh God." Forty-five minutes later, I sat up in bed, wrapped the sheet around my naked torso, and gazed over at Jeff. "That was, um . . ."

"Don't say it," he warned. "I don't want your pity."

I cleared my throat and tried to be tactful. "Okay, but can I just—"

"Don't!" His blue eyes flashed angrily. "We are never going to speak of this again!"

"But . . . I think we *have* to talk about it."

"No." He leapt out of bed and turned his back on me while he struggled into his jeans, getting tangled in the cuffs and falling to the floor with a crash that rattled the window. *"Shit."* In his frustration, he groped for the nearest solid object—one of my high-heeled sandals—and hurled it against the wall, where it left a dent in the plaster.

"Nice." I nodded at the culmination at what had become the worst evening of my entire life. "Now my bedroom is as bruised as your ego. Does that make you feel better?"

"No." He slammed his fist against the carpet.

I switched on the desk lamp next to the bed. "Listen, Jeff. This isn't that big a deal. Swear to God—"

"Don't even!" he cut me off. "Don't try to pretend it doesn't matter. Don't try to make me feel better. You can't possibly understand what this feels like. It's every guy's worst fucking nightmare."

I bowed my head, wishing I could erase the fumbling embarrassment of the last half hour. "Well, it's not exactly my dream scenario, either."

"Can we please stop talking about this? I'm gonna go back to Quentin's place and kill myself if you don't shut up!"

"*You're* going to kill yourself?" I flopped back down against the mattress. "How do you think I feel? This is the second time tonight I've been completely rejected."

He absolutely lost it, flinging the sandal's mate into the closet wall. *"I did not reject you!* This isn't about you."

"Uh, I beg to differ. I seem to remember being an active participant."

"Yeah, but . . ." He exhaled, a long, sputtering sigh of disgust. "You can't understand."

"It's me, isn't it? I'm physically repulsive to guys."

"It's not you, okay? It's me. Me and my pathetic, traitorous, useless body."

But I knew the truth. "I'm a walking, talking man repellant. Maybe this lingerie is lined with kryptonite?"

"Would you stop it? I already feel bad enough without having to apologize every fifteen seconds. You know you're hot as hell."

"Then why am I still an eighteen-year-old virgin?"

"Oh, boo frigging hoo! At least your equipment works!"

We were both feeling too sorry for ourselves to feel sorry for each other.

"Maybe you're right," I finally said. "Maybe we should never speak of this again."

"Agreed," Jeff told the floor. He hadn't made eye contact since the, um, unfortunate deflation occurred.

I tried to sound cheery. "And I know this was a little weird, but we can always try again, right?"

"You're offering me mercy sex?!?" He stood up and grabbed his shirt off the dresser. "That's it. I'm leaving."

I nodded, my darkest suspicions confirmed. "So you *are* repulsed by me! It's my upper arms, isn't it?" I scowled down at the offending appendages. "My upper arms nauseate you."

"I'm leaving," he repeated, buttoning up his shirt. "I'm getting on the next flight back to Massachusetts."

"But I thought you were staying till next weekend?"

"Not after this, I'm not!"

"You're serious?"

He tucked his shirttails into his jeans and headed for the door. " 'Bye."

"But we're still friends, right?"

He hesitated way too long before replying, "Sure."

"Yeah." I nodded sadly. "That's what I thought."

" 'Bye," he said softly, not even facing me.

" 'Bye," I whispered as he pulled the bedroom door shut behind him.

I listened to his footsteps retreating down the hall, then the dead bolt turning downstairs, then the front door opening and closing.

Then nothing. Jeff was gone, along with thirteen years of friendship.

So far, I was finding sex to be *highly* overrated.

12

"Nice going with Jeff last night." Jacinda took a gulp of coffee as she sat down at the kitchen table the next morning. "Why didn't you just cut off his balls and throw them in your makeup bag along with your mascara and lipstick?"

"The hell?" I grabbed a carton of orange juice and slammed the refrigerator door. "How do you know about that?"

"The great and powerful Jacinda knows all," she assured me with a Cheshire cat smile.

"No, seriously." Heat flooded into my cheeks. "Do you have my room bugged? Are you so bored that you have nothing to do but spy on me?"

She took a bite of her chocolate croissant and rolled her eyes. "Okay, first of all, if I ever got so bored that spying on Sister Eva Chastity sounded interesting, I'd probably slip into a coma—"

"Oh, that's right," I snapped. "You decided to screw Coelle's man to entertain yourself."

"Shut up," she hissed, glancing toward the stairs.

"What? You only want to brag about poaching her boyfriend to *me*?"

She tossed her hair. "I didn't brag about anything; you cornered me and made me talk!"

"Whatever helps you sleep at night." I poured myself a glass of juice and glared at her. "Now how did you find out about me and Jeff?"

"Listen, babe, I know you're new to this, so I'll give you a few pointers." Her voice dripped with condescension. "Tip number one: The penis is a very sensitive little flower. Ego-crushing criticism tends to make it shrivel up and die."

I clamped my hands over my ears and sang "The Star-Spangled Banner" at the top of my lungs until her lips stopped moving.

"What?" She grinned. "You don't want advice from an expert? Lots of people would pay good money for this. I could make a fortune giving seminars."

"How did you find out about me and Jeff?" I repeated.

She raised an eyebrow. "Tip number two: It is considered bad form to sleep with two guys in one night. That's a little extreme, even for me."

I closed my eyes. "I didn't have sex with Danny last night."

"You didn't?"

"No, we had a giant fight in the hotel room—about Jeff, actually—and he had a hissy fit and stormed out and when I came home Jeff was waiting for me and—"

She held up a hand. "Let me get this straight. You got into bed with two guys last night and you *still* haven't gone all the way?"

"I'm going to be a virgin forever," I moaned. "I'm cursed."

"Girl, you are hopeless." She unfolded the morning edition of *South of Sunset.*

"I'll ask you one more time before I take that croissant away," I warned. "How did you find out about me and Jeff?"

She shoved half the remaining pastry into her mouth and mumbled, "I ran into him in the courtyard last night. He looked like death in baggy jeans."

I cringed. "Right after we . . . ?"

"Yep. He was totally freaked out. Poor thing actually thought he could flag down a cab on La Cienega. I was like, sweetie, this isn't Manhattan."

"Oh God. Do you think he got back to Quentin's okay?"

"I know he did." The Cheshire cat smile was back.

I narrowed my eyes. "What is that supposed to mean?"

"I did you a favor. Drove him back to Quentin's so he could pack up his stuff. I had to wait outside, naturally, in case Coelle was up there—"

"Naturally."

"—And then I drove him to LAX and listened to his tale of woe."

I choked on my OJ. "He *told* you what happened when we . . . ?"

"Not exactly. But I could read between the lines. He was mortified, absolutely mortified. He really wanted to impress you with his manly skills. I felt so sorry for him."

I heaved a huge sigh of relief. "Well, as long as he got home safe."

"So I made a man of him. Then I bought him a ticket for the red-eye to Boston so he could go home early."

I blinked. "You 'made a man of him'?"

She nodded, rolling up the sleeves of her red silk kimono. "Uh-huh. The backseat of my Benz is roomier than it looks."

"Jacinda!"

"What? One of us had to get the job done! And you didn't want him, anyway."

"But . . ." I couldn't stop blinking. "You barely even know him!"

"Exactly. Made it much easier for the poor kid. With you, there was a whole lifetime of pressure built up."

"What is the matter with you?" I sputtered. "Is it your life's mission to sleep with every single guy Coelle and I have ever met?"

"Okay, instead of berating me and being all judgmental, you should be begging me to help you sort out your sorry excuse for a sex life."

"But . . ." I threw up my hands. "Fine. What should I do

about Danny? Should I tell him about what happened with Jeff?"

Her head snapped up. "No. That's an easy, one-word answer. The less he knows, the better."

"But the guilt!" I wailed. "It's eating me up inside."

"Why? You didn't actually do anything with Jeff. There was no official sex, right?"

"No, but I *would've* if I could've. That's the same as actually having sex with him, kind of."

"Not in my world."

"What am I going to do? I have to tell him."

"No, you do not." She gave me a no-nonsense, war general look. "Listen to me, Eva. I've been in this situation: hell, I'm in it right now with you-know-who." She glanced up toward Coelle's bedroom. "I know what I'm talking about."

"But—"

"Have you told anyone else about what happened last night?"

I shook my head. "It's between you, me, and the coffee cup. Oh, and Jeff, of course."

"Well, he's on a flight back to the other side of the country." She put down her mug with a definitive *thunk.* "So here's what you do: Keep your big mouth shut. Don't tell anyone else about this. Don't even think about it, if you can help it. Pretend the whole thing never happened."

"I can't."

"Yes, you can! Look how easy!" She pantomimed zipping her lips, locking them with an imaginary key, and tossing the key over her shoulder. "Ta-da, your problems are solved!"

"But even if I ignore the whole thing—which I'm still not convinced is the right thing to do—"

"I'd err on the side of keeping your boyfriend. Assuming you still want him, of course."

"I do want him. But I have to tell him." A sickening sense of dread seeped into my stomach. "My whole life has been built on lies. My mother, my aunt, my grandparents—it's been nothing but lies since I came out of the womb. I don't want my relationship with Danny to be built on lies, too."

"But you're not lying to him!" She slugged back the last of her coffee. "You're just . . . conveniently forgetting to mention a few things."

"Omission is the same as a lie."

"I'm gonna throw up my croissant if you keep preaching."

I raised an eyebrow. "You do what you have to do with Coelle and I'll do what I have to do with Danny."

"Fine. But we keep each other's secrets, right?"

"Sure."

"Under pain of death, right?"

"Whatever."

"I mean it, Eva." She looked me in the eye. "We'll keep each other's secrets."

"Deal. But I still think you should tell Coelle."

"Yeah, well, you keep thinking that. By the way, you're in the paper again."

I snatched *South of Sunset* from Jacinda's outstretched hand. "Not again!"

THE G-SPOT WITH GIGI GELTIN

My spies tell me that washed-up super-model Marisela Cordes is desperately attempting to stay in the spotlight, making a scene wherever she can, even though she's been banned from every studio soundstage in town. The latest explosion of theatrics went down at the car wash on La Cienega. High noon. Marisela and look-alike daughter Eva waged a take-no-prisoners war of words in front of a gaggle of goggling onlook-ers. "It was vicious," reports one en-thralled SUV owner. "They were carrying on about money, sex, abor-tions. It was like a scene from the tack-iest reality show ever." Speaking of tacky, I hear little Eva's ride was more FedEx van than fabulous. Looks like Marisela, who's trying to win back boy toy financier Tyson O'Donnell, better tell her kid that stylish is as stylish does!

*   *   *

The tiny metal ridges on the bleacher seats dug into my thighs as I stared at the sweaty college boys sprinting all over the baseball diamond. I leaned forward, rested my elbows on my knees, and checked my watch. Danny's team practice had already stretched well past an hour, and so far he'd barely looked my way. But he knew I was here—we'd made eye contact when I first showed up, after which he immediately disappeared into the dugout for ten minutes. Well, he could run but he couldn't hide. We were *having* this conversation.

Jacinda was right: Telling the truth about Jeff was a huge risk. But if Danny and I were going to start fresh, I had to be honest.

And if he decided to break up with me in the middle of the baseball diamond, well . . . that's what I deserved, right?

After what seemed like decades, Danny finally waved off the catcher, rubbed his left shoulder, and stepped down from the pitcher's mound.

I got to my feet and made my way down to the field. That's when the cleat chaser showed up. Short and skinny, with dyed hair that had more roots than a Canadian Christmas tree farm, she bounced out of the dugout and started stroking Danny's biceps. Right in front of me.

I rolled my eyes as she reached up to readjust the brim of his baseball cap; I fully expected him to pull away. But he didn't. He let her keep pawing him.

"Hey!" I yelled.

He pretended not to hear me, but I was pretty hard to miss, marching across the infield with my fists balled at my sides, ready to rip out a few chunks of that ho biscuit's badly bleached hair.

The blonde giggled, murmured something that I didn't quite catch, then leaned in toward Danny while literally licking her lips. He laughed and tilted his head toward her.

She kissed him. He kissed her back.

I gaped with open-mouthed horror, feeling like someone had dumped a vat of icy postgame Gatorade on me.

When he finally came up for air, he glanced back at me with a triumphant smile. "Oh, hi, Eva."

Where were all the baseball bats when I needed them? "What the hell was that?"

He tried to look nonchalant. "You said you didn't want me to be so boring."

I reeled backward, debating whether I should slap him or the groupie. "You're a pig!"

"Well, better a pig than a balding, suburban accountant." He sounded proud of himself. "Who's thirty-five now?"

13

"So did you slap him?" Jacinda demanded over dinner at Kalva, an organic, vegetarian restaurant near our apartment. We were dining al fresco on the sidewalk patio, some of us chowing down more enthusiastically than others.

"Of course not." I sniffed suspiciously at the green miso soup the waiter had just put in front of me. "I wanted to, though. I had violence in my soul, I tell you. Violence in my soul."

"You should have punched his pitching arm." Coelle, who had picked the restaurant, closed her eyes as she savored her grilled tofu sandwich. "He deserves to have his rotator cuff ripped in half for what he did to you."

Jacinda and I exchanged a meaningful look. I had told Coelle about the argument with Danny at the Somerset Hotel, but not about the aftermath with Jeff in my bedroom. I was shocked that Jacinda could actually keep a secret, but I guess she had a vested interest in being discreet: if she blew my cover, I'd blow hers.

"I don't know," I hedged. "I said some pretty harsh stuff to him on Saturday."

But Coelle was having none of this. "Don't you dare make excuses for him. Who cares what you said? He *kissed* someone else! Right in front of you! That's unforgivable."

"Plus, using the old 'make you jealous by kissing some random hoochie' routine?" Jacinda shook her head. "Talk about unoriginal."

I looked up from my miso soup. "You really think he was just trying to make me jealous?"

"Duh! Why else would he start sucking face with Superfan Barbie right in front of you? *Trés* tacky."

"Not to mention passive-aggressive and desperate," Coelle added.

The violence in my soul receded just a little. "So you don't think he actually likes her?"

"Please." Jacinda scoffed. "Going from you to her would be like trading in a Ferrari for a Hyundai."

"But who cares if he likes her or not?" Coelle shoved her tofu aside and started lecturing me like a high school guidance counselor. "Swapping spit with some other girl is never okay. He stepped way over the line."

"I know," I muttered.

"And he violated your trust! Kissing is cheating in my book."

So was trying to have sex with another guy. "I know."

"So? Who wants to date a cheater? I wouldn't ever speak to him again, if I were you. He lies, he cheats, he uses skankalicious groupies to make his point instead of having an adult discussion . . . forget it. I won't tolerate *friends* lying to me, forget boyfriends. If one of you guys started making out with Quentin—"

"I have to go to the bathroom," Jacinda announced, throwing her napkin on her chair as she raced inside.

Coelle snapped out of her tirade long enough to frown at our roommate's retreating back and ask, "What's with her?"

"Maybe the lime-cilantro dressing didn't agree with her?" I suggested, trying to sound innocent.

She shook her head. "I had that on my salad and it was delicious. Anyway, forget him. You can do a thousand times better than Danny Bristow. He's just a dumb jock."

I pushed the broccoli garnish around the soup bowl with my spoon. Danny wasn't a dumb jock. He was sweet and funny and smart—and, oh yeah, searingly hot—and he was the only guy in the 310 area code I wanted to date. Sure, I was mad that he kissed someone else, but when I thought about what I'd tried to do with Jeff . . .

"Eva?" Coelle tapped my hand with her drinking straw. "Hello?"

I looked up, blinking. "Yeah?"

"I just asked you if you want to tag along with me and Quentin tonight." The wattage in her smile increased at the mere mention of his name. "We're going to another benefit ball. I'm wearing this supersexy zebra-print dress and these diamond earrings that my publicist convinced Cathy Waterman to loan me . . ."

"Hold on." I checked under the table to make sure she was still wearing the usual jeans and running shoes with her bulky Cornell sweatshirt. "*You're* going to wear a supersexy zebra-print dress? Of your own free will?"

"I've decided I kind of like dressing up." She grinned. "Quentin likes it when women show a little skin. I got the wardrobe lady on the set to give me some tips. She said I have great cleavage and I should accent it."

Danny was smooching the ho biscuit, Coelle was playing up her boobs . . . it was official: the world was going to hell in a Dior handbag. "So you really like him, huh?" I asked carefully.

"Yeah. I feel like I could just talk to him for hours," she said, her eyes glazing over with bliss. "I kind of blew him off at first, but now . . . he really *understands* me, you know? He doesn't like me because I'm the jailbait chick from *Twilight's Tempest.* He likes me for who I really am."

I chose my words carefully. "But you seem so much more intellectual than he is. I mean, you're Ivy League material."

"Don't be a snob," she admonished. "Just because I'm serious about my education doesn't mean I want to date stuck-up, boring Mensa guys. I didn't have a normal childhood—I grew up on film sets. And so did he. Once we started talking, we had this instant bond. I can't even explain it."

"Well, just be careful," I cautioned. "Don't rush into anything."

"Eva." Her smile was patronizing. "Just because your boyfriend cheated on you doesn't mean that mine will. I know what I'm doing. I'm very mature for my age, remember? And I'm happy. Finally. I've stopped obsessing about every tiny, little detail of life."

She *had* seemed more balanced lately. Like today—she was actually ingesting food and talking about something besides the SAT. "Okay," I relented. "You're probably right. I should just stay out of it."

"Yes, you should, because he's going to be a big part of my life from now on." She lowered her voice. "I may be doing some lingerie shopping of my own in the very near future."

"You're going to have sex with him?" I yelled as a noisy city bus trundled up to the curb.

She shot me a dirty look and waited until the bus pulled away before whispering, "Maybe tonight. The zebra-print dress is a preview."

"But don't you think you should hold off until you get to know him better?" I protested. "Aren't you moving a little fast?"

She shrugged. "I can't help myself. When I'm with him, I feel . . . free. I'm eighteen years old and I'm just now learning to have fun. I deserve a break from all the bullshit and I don't care what anybody thinks." She leaned back in her chair and crossed her arms, defying me to challenge her.

"You do deserve a break. I know. But just . . . be careful, okay?"

She laughed and waved to Jacinda, who had emerged from

the ladies' room. "I've been careful my whole life. I'm overdue for a little adventure."

"What are we talking about?" Jacinda picked at an invisible stain on her cream wool skirt as she took her seat across from Coelle.

"Quentin," Coelle replied with a dreamy sigh.

"Still?" Jacinda looked distressed. "Can't you two ever talk about anything but boys? Jeez, ladies, expand your horizons."

Coelle laughed. "This from the biggest flirt on the West Coast?"

"And the East Coast," I added. "And Europe."

"I'm just sick and tired of talking about guys," Jacinda grumbled. "Is that such a crime? Let's move on."

"Fine. What would you like to discuss?" Coelle asked.

"How about dinner? Tofu makes me retch and I'm starving to death. Everyone who wants to hit the drive-thru on the way home say 'aye.'"

"Aye." I raised my hand.

"Don't come crying to me when you get all kinds of nasty cancers and heart disease," Coelle warned.

"Tell you what: they can bury me in a giant french fry carton instead of a coffin and you can give a eulogy on the dangers of saturated fat." She grabbed her buckle-riddled black purse and looked expectantly at us. "Ready to go?"

"Fine." Coelle took a few final bites of her sandwich and flagged down the server for our check. "But someday you're going to be exposed for the chav in debutante's clothing you are, and when that day comes, I'm going to laugh my ass off."

"Au contraire," Jacinda trilled. "If the press found out I live to supersize, I'd be refreshingly down-to-earth. Unpretentious. Now, if they found out the same thing about Eva, *she'd* be a chav."

"Hey!" I protested.

"Sorry, babe. I was born into the old-money elite; you come from social-climber stock. It's a genetic crapshoot and you lost. Enjoy your tofu."

Coelle examined the bill and handed the waiter a credit card. "So Eva, you coming tonight?"

I wrinkled my nose. "Nah, I have to track down my mom and my aunt and torture them until they tell me who Thomas is and what happened to him." As her eyes widened, I summarized what had happened at the car wash.

"Your life is like an issue of the *National Enquirer*," she marveled when I finished. "Well, have fun with the cross-examination. Do you really think you might have a little brother out there?"

"Who knows?" I handed her a twenty to cover my portion of the bill. "Knowing my mom, Thomas is probably a five-headed alien baby with ESP and eyes that shoot lasers."

Coelle gave my arm a consolatory pat, then turned to Jacinda. "What about you? Any interest in coming with me and Quentin to a charity thing tonight?"

Jacinda gagged like she'd just pounded back a bushel of brussels sprouts. "No thanks. I'm busy. Very busy."

"Oh, c'mon," Coelle cajoled. "You're always saying you're

bored with no boyfriend. There'll be tons of hot guys at this event. You can dress up, slather on way too much eye makeup, it'll be fun."

"Love to, but I can't. I have a thing I have to go to. A, um, very important thing."

Coelle planted both hands on her hips and gave Jacinda a piercing stare. "Is this about Quentin?"

"No! Why would you even say that?"

"Ever since the *Buzzkill* party, you've freaked out every time I say his name." Coelle's big, soulful eyes had narrowed to cynical little slits. "What's going on?"

"Nothing!" Jacinda yelped. "Nothing!"

"Listen, if you have a problem with my boyfriend—"

"I don't! No problem! I think he's great," Jacinda swore, tugging the neck of her cashmere sweater up around her chin. "Just peachy."

Coelle gave her a long, accusatory look. "I know what's going on."

Jacinda's mouth disappeared into the sweater. "You . . . you do?"

Coelle nodded. "I'm not as stupid as you think."

I backed up a few steps, planning my escape route for when the hair pulling and eye gouging began.

"Listen." Jacinda held up both her palms. "Don't jump to any hasty conclusions. I can explain—"

"You can't stand that any guy would like me more than you," Coelle accused. "You expect everyone to fall at your feet and if I get one single, solitary boy for myself, your ego goes berserk."

Jacinda let her hands drop. "Uh . . ."

"I've known you for two years and finally—*finally!*—a guy worth dating is attracted to me instead of you and you can't stand it!"

Jacinda shrugged one shoulder. "You know me . . . jealous, petty . . . it's just my way."

"Well, grow up. Even if you can't forgive Quentin for liking me instead of you—not that you even want him, you narcissist—you should at least suck it up and be civil to him."

I looked at Jacinda. Jacinda looked at me. Then she turned to Coelle and said, with a humility I didn't know she was capable of, "You're right. I guess I need to get over myself."

Coelle was shocked into speechlessness by this response.

"I'll try to be nice to Quentin, I really will." She did an Oscar-worthy rendition of holding back tears.

"Oh, Jacinda!" Coelle engulfed her in a big, nurturing hug. "I forgive you. I know you're trying! But you can't base your whole sense of self-worth on boys. It's just not healthy."

"We can't all be as strong as you," Jacinda ground out. "But I'll work on it. And I hope you and Quentin are happy together, for real."

"We are!" Coelle got that crazed love-junkie look in her eyes again. "Maybe someday you can be a bridesmaid at our wedding."

While Jacinda's Mercedes idled at the drive-thru, I dialed up my mom, who completely shocked me by picking up. Guess Laurel's guesthouse didn't have caller ID.

"It's me," I announced.

"Oh. You." Her tone went frosty. "What do you want?"

"Tell me about Thomas," I demanded.

She gulped audibly. "Who . . . where did you hear about him?"

"Aunt Laurel told me everything," I lied. "So don't bother trying to hide the truth."

"Laurel *told you?*" She sounded as betrayed as I felt. Excellent.

"Yep. I asked a few leading questions and she sang like an *American Idol* reject. So cut the crap, Mom. I know what's up."

"Why are you doing this to me?" She sounded like she was down to her last nerve. "You accuse me of horrible parenting right in front of my boyfriend, you side with that ruthless bitch Daphne Farnsworth over me, and now you're going to bring up the Thomas situation?"

"That 'situation,' as you so delicately put it, is my flesh and blood. And since you and Laurel live to screw with me and the Farnsworths clearly want me dead, Thomas is my last chance for a normal family member." I had gone pretty far out on a limb with that one; I held my breath and crossed my fingers, praying she wouldn't call my bluff.

"You don't love me anymore, do you?" She drew in a long shaky breath. "I knew you'd hate me when you found out, but I did what I thought was the right thing."

"What? What did you do?" I demanded so loudly that Jacinda spilled her soda all over herself.

"I can't have this conversation over the phone," my mother whispered. "I have to see you."

"I'm sorry; could you repeat that? It sounded like you said you actually *want* to see me."

"Of course I want to see you, baby girl. I always want to see you."

I managed not to laugh. "Whatever."

"Let's get together tonight. We'll have dinner, go shopping, do some mother-daughter bonding."

"I think we're about fifteen years too late for that," I snitted.

"Eva . . ." Long, put-upon sigh. "I'm trying, okay? I really want to make up for some of the time we lost. So could you please stop with the hostility for one night? I'm offering to buy you clothes—*pretend* to be grateful."

Hmm. I did like clothes. "Okay, Mommy, let's bond."

"I can't wait." She could not have sounded less enthusiastic. "You know how to get to the Grove, right? Meet me outside Anthropologie at six-thirty."

14

I arrived at the Grove with plenty of time to spare and increasingly mixed feelings because this shopping center, in addition to being a hip 'n' happening hangout, was the site of my first date with Danny. We had been so happy that night, so excited just to be together.

There was the farmers' market where we'd held hands and looked for the cheesiest souvenir in all of Southern California. The pizza stall where we'd shared a calorie fest, the aftermath of which still remained on my upper arms. The movie theater where Danny had gotten a fat lip while having a fistfight with C Money. *Aww.*

I inhaled deeply, choking on the sudden lungful of L.A.

smog, and wished I could redo everything that had come after that fateful first date. I'd buy a leather thong like Jacinda's, I'd keep my trap shut when I seduced Danny, and most of all, I'd refuse to let Jeff Oerte into my apartment. Ever.

Once I located Anthropologie, I did a little anticipatory browsing (that purple strapless dress in the window would look great in my closet), then checked my watch: 6:25. My mom never showed up anywhere on time—that was against her religion—so I took a seat on one of the large wooden benches lining the shopping center's cobblestone plaza and waited.

And waited.

And waited.

After another two hours and about a hundred fruitless phone calls to my mom's cellphone (which she had obviously turned off), I accepted the fact that I had once again been callously ditched by the woman who'd given birth to me.

Not that I accepted this gracefully—I allowed myself a silent but hysterical meltdown on my cold little bench. I watched the carefree shoppers bustle by, absolutely consumed with envy. I *so* wanted to be one of the impossibly tan, thin L.A. girls sashaying out of Anthropologie, insulated against the real world by Gucci sunglasses and Daddy's credit cards. These untouchable Teflon blondes probably had parents who loved them, boyfriends who would never even glance at a groupie, girlfriends who didn't embroil them in Hollywood hazing ordeals and boyfriend-stealing subterfuge.

As my jealousy and disappointment gelled into a cold, hard fury, I saw a familiar figure walking toward me.

"Danny? What are you doing here?"

He stopped a few feet away from the bench and rocked back on his heels. "Your mom called me. She said you'd be waiting for her and you might want some company."

Please let me have heard that wrong. "My *mom* called you?"

He nodded. "About forty-five minutes ago."

"Wait." I wrinkled up my forehead. "How did she get your number? How does she even *know* about you?"

He sounded hurt. "You didn't tell your mom about me?"

"Of course not! I actually like you—or I *did,* anyway. Why would I tell her about you? She'd just find a way to mess everything up."

"Well, I guess she called the apartment and told Jacinda that she wasn't going to be able to meet you, and Jacinda suggested she call me."

Damn you, Crane-Laird! "Typical. She didn't have the guts to call me herself, so instead she's dragging all my friends in to do her dirty work."

He took a step closer to me. "You really shouldn't be so hard on her, Eva. She's doing the best she can."

The expression on my face must have made him realize his error because he immediately started to backpedal. "Look, I know I should probably stay out of it—"

"Yeah." My voice was high and clipped. "You should."

"—but she said she had a dire emergency and even though she really wanted to see you—"

"And you believed her?" Unable to contain my frustration, I leapt to my feet and started pacing back and forth. "An emergency? Give me a break."

"She really did sound upset," he said defensively. "She was crying and everything. I'm sure she'd be here if she could."

"She was crying because she had to be on the phone with you instead of dancing on the bar at Mood! I guarantee the pathetic little sniffles dried up about half a second after she hung up." I'd hoped that venting would calm me down, but it had the opposite effect: the more I yelled, the more I *wanted* to yell.

"And anyway, why are you even here? Shouldn't you be getting a hickey from your new girlfriend right about now?"

He didn't have anything to say to that.

"I mean it, Danny! What the hell? When I try to talk to you about what happened at the hotel last weekend, you blow me off. But when my *mom* calls, you drop everything and run right over?"

"Well." He stopped squinting at the storefront and looked at me. "I screwed up. I admit it. I'm sorry."

"I'm sorry, too!" I flared. "I'm sorry that you treated both me and your little cleat chaser like crap. I'm sorry that you'd rather take my mom's side than mine. I'm sorry that we ever had a date at this stupid farmers' market because now it's ruined forever for me!"

He looked like I'd just punched him in the stomach.

"What?" I demanded, so hurt by his betrayal, and by my mother's, that I wanted to make him suffer the way I was suffering. I sort of forgot about the whole Jeff indiscretion for a minute and let my anger take over.

"Nothing," he said quietly. "I came out here to see if you wanted to talk."

"No, you didn't! You came out here because my mother told you to, and just like every other man she meets, you dropped everything to go do her bidding."

"This is about you, Eva. Not your mother. I'm here because I want to talk about—"

Perilously close to tears, I drew myself up to my full height and glared at him. "Nothing you say is going to make any difference."

"So that's it?" His eyes were dark. "We're done?"

I nodded slowly. "I just can't stand to be disappointed by one more person I love."

He paused. *"This* is how you tell me you love me, too?"

I couldn't bring myself to answer this question. I just turned on my heel and walked away before he could see me cry.

Eight hours later, I tossed and turned on my tiny twin bed, unable to get comfortable. The soft glow from the streetlights filtered in through the vertical blinds, but the light wasn't the reason I couldn't sleep. All I could think about was the look in Danny's eyes when I'd accidentally admitted I loved him. What had gone wrong with us? Why did I wait until our whole relationship had turned into a SigAlert on the 405 freeway (aka a smoldering, multicar pileup of charred, twisted metal) to realize I loved him?

I pondered this into the wee hours of the morning, when Coelle stumbled in the front door with Quentin and proceeded to make noise. A lot of noise. Noise of the giggling, gasping, and moaning variety. Apparently, the zebra-print dress had lived up to its promise. I clamped a pillow over my head, closed my eyes, and tried to sleep, but two hours later, I was still wide awake and Coelle and Quentin were louder than ever.

"Morning," Coelle whispered when I met her at the door to the bathroom at 6:30 A.M. She was wearing her Cornell sweatshirt and nothing else. "What are you doing up so early?"

"I have a breakfast meeting with my aunt. What about you? Early call on the set?"

"I have to be in makeup by eight." She grinned. "They're gonna have to use a ton of undereye concealer, 'cause I got, like, zero sleep last night."

"Really," I said dryly. "I never would've guessed."

"Yeah, Quentin and I had a great time at the benefit ball and then we went to this new club in Los Feliz, and when he dropped me off, he walked me to the door . . . and he's still here!" Her big brown eyes gleamed. "We *did* it!"

I tried to look surprised. "Wow. How was it?"

She clasped her hand over her heart and collapsed against the wall. "So great! He is so in love with me, Eva, I swear. Remember how I said we had a connection? Well, last night—"

"What are you guys whispering about?" Jacinda's tousled blonde head popped out of her doorway. "And why are you whispering loud enough to wake me up?"

"Sorry." I glanced at Coelle's door, hoping Quentin

wouldn't come bursting out and see Jacinda in the tank top and glittery G-string she considered pajamas. "Quentin spent the night, and he's still here, so . . ."

"Oh. Okay. Good night." Jacinda jerked her head back into her room and locked the door behind her.

"What a hag." Coelle strode over to the door and started pounding away. "Jacinda. Jacinda? You said you were going to be *nice* to him, remember?"

"I am being nice," came the muffled response. "Not coming out of here until I've had four more hours of sleep and a triple espresso is the nicest thing I can do."

"Don't give me that! Put on some clothes and have breakfast with us."

No answer. I imagined her barricading the door with her dresser, mattress, and several seasons' worth of designer outfits.

"Jacinda . . ." *Knock, knock, knock.*

"Maybe we should just leave her alone," I suggested. "She's a beast if she doesn't get her beauty sleep."

"This isn't about beauty sleep! This is about her being snotty to my boyfriend just because he likes me better than her."

"I already said I'd be nice to your stupid boyfriend," Jacinda retorted from the other side of her door. "But I'm physically incapable of being nice to anyone before the sun comes up, so don't push your luck!"

"Listen, missy, I'm going downstairs to make cinnamon rolls and you better be down there—wearing pants—in exactly fifteen minutes. Or else . . ."

"Or else what?" I asked.

"Or else she can find herself a new roommate." Coelle glared mutinously at the closed door. "If she can't make small talk for ten minutes and choke down some pastry, I'll know she doesn't really value my friendship."

Silence from Jacinda.

"Do you hear me?" Coelle pressed. "The clock is ticking."

More silence.

I cracked under the pressure. "Jacinda! Please!"

Big sigh from behind the barricade. "What kind of cinnamon rolls?"

"Pillsbury," Coelle replied. "Quentin's favorite."

"Not even homemade?" Jacinda whined.

"When I sleep with you, I'll make your favorite," Coelle retorted. "Until then, you'll eat Pillsbury and like it."

I changed into sweats and brushed my hair before coming down to the cinnamon-scented kitchen and taking my place at the little round table, which Coelle had set with paper napkins and a huge glass pitcher of orange juice.

"Wow," I commented. "How home ec."

Coelle laughed, dumping a few scoops of French Roast into the coffeemaker. "I know. Sex brings out the Martha Stewart in me. Maybe it's hormones—the urge to nest and all that."

I wondered if sex would make me want to nest, too. Would I have wanted to get out of bed and knit a pair of wool socks for Danny? Or bake a pie? I saw myself as more of the lying-around-in-the-afterglow-eating-bonbons-and-watching-bad-TV-with-my-beloved type, but I'd probably never know for sure, seeing as I was *doomed to be a virgin forever.*

Coelle pulled a tray of steaming cinnamon rolls out of the oven, smothered them with white glaze from a plastic tub, and piled them onto a plate.

"Breakfast is served," she announced as Quentin made his way down the stairs, tugging at the bottom of his blue plaid boxer shorts and rubbing his stubbly chin. *"Bon appétit."*

"Hey, babe, thanks." Quentin helped himself to a roll, ate it over the sink, and yanked the coffeepot off the steaming boilerplate, oblivious to the sizzling drops of coffee still dripping out of the filter funnel.

Good thing he looked like Jake Gyllenhaal, 'cause he could never make it on charm and good manners.

"Morning, campers." Jacinda sauntered in, looking almost frumpy. She had scraped her hair back into a tight ponytail and covered her entire body in baggy, plaid flannel pants and a bulky, pink terry-cloth robe. "Smells divine in here, but since when do you bake?"

"Since when do you wear flannel?" Coelle shot back. "I thought you'd break out in hives in anything that isn't imported from Paris."

"The real question is, since when do you eat cinnamon rolls?" I stared as Coelle licked the icing off her fingers.

She lifted her chin. "Just because I don't mainline processed sugar all day doesn't mean I don't like sweets. Everything in moderation, that's my motto."

"What? Since when is that your motto?" I snorted.

"Jacinda," Coelle said, pointedly changing the subject. "Aren't you going to say hi to Quentin?"

"Hi," Jacinda muttered, sticking her head into the refrigerator. "What . . . I mean, why . . . I mean, how are you?"

"Awesome." He smiled a heartbreaking smile at Coelle, who dissolved into a mushy, blushy mess. "How're you?"

"Couldn't be better." Jacinda chugged a cold can of Red Bull, looking at me with a mixture of panic and disgust.

"Hi," I greeted Quentin, but no one paid any attention to me.

"I've got to run." Coelle glanced at the digital clock on the microwave, then kissed Quentin on the cheek. "What time are you going to be at the set, sweetie?"

"Like ten, ten-thirty? I don't have any scenes until the afternoon, so I was thinking I might hit the tanning booth and the gym."

I'd heard Coelle go off on twenty-minute rants about the evils of carcinoma and the idiocy of people (like Jacinda) who courted tanning-booth skin cancer, but today she just giggled and dragged Quentin to the door so he could say good-bye properly.

"Last night was incredible," Coelle cooed. "Call me when you're on your way to work, okay?"

"Okay." His voice was a verbal shrug. "See you later."

"You'll miss me, right?" she wheedled.

"Sure."

Jacinda pretended to throw up in the sink.

When Coelle finally managed to tear herself away,

Quentin shut the door behind her and ambled back to the table. "These are good," he remarked, grabbing another cinnamon roll before turning to Jacinda. "So what's up?"

She folded her arms over her chest. "Why didn't you tell me you were interested in Coelle before you had sex with me?"

"Coelle?" He blinked in confusion. "Oh, we're not serious."

"Yes, you are!" She leapt to her feet, jabbing her fork toward his genitalia. "You'd better be serious about her! *Dead* serious!"

"But . . ." he retreated to the living room, putting the overstuffed lavender couch between him and the fork. "We're just having fun."

"Listen up, Rico Suave: you stopped 'just having fun' when you let that"—she pointed to the offending body part with her fork—"loose in her bedroom. You're her boyfriend now and so help me God, you'd better be monogamous. If you hurt her . . ."

"Hey. Cindy." He chuckled but, I noticed, kept his distance from the flatware. "What are you freaking about? Don't worry about me and Coelle."

"You did not just call me Cindy!" Jacinda looked like she was about to trade her fork for a meat cleaver.

"Yeah." Quentin gave her an impish wink. "It's like my pet name for you."

"My name is Jacinda! Jacinda! Do you hear me?"

"Whoa." He backed up a few more steps. "Calm down, okay? What's your problem? I didn't do anything."

"Actually, you did me *and* my roommate. That's my problem. And it's gonna be your problem if you mess this up."

Quentin appealed to me with wounded, puppy-dog eyes. "All I did was—"

"Hey!" Jacinda wasn't through yet. "You'd better treat Coelle like a princess. And if you say anything about what happened between you and me . . ." She let her gaze linger first on the fork, then on his crotch.

"I get it, I get it." He cupped his hands protectively over his fly. "Wow, you actresses are always so, like, intense."

"Just keep your mouth shut and your pants zipped." Jacinda's smile was sharp and dangerous. "Or else."

15

"So. Eva." My aunt draped her white linen napkin in her lap and studied the breakfast menu at Sojo. "We have lots to talk about."

"Yes, we do." I'd spruced up a bit before piloting the Goose over to Beverly Hills—given Jacinda's casual air about discarding her couture, I'd become just as casual about claiming her castoffs as my own. Today I'd paired her rust-colored Luca Luca blazer with my own Old Navy jeans. Call me eclectic.

"Marisela tells me you confronted her about Thomas." She straightened the lapels of her black suit.

"Did she also tell you that she agreed to meet me at the

Grove and then stood me up?" I reached into the bread basket and grabbed a tiny lemon-poppyseed muffin. As long as I had already gone into carb overload with Coelle's cinnamon rolls, I might as well keep going, right?

"Cast your mind back to the day you arrived in L.A." Laurel paused to signal to the waiter that we were ready to order. "Did I or did I not warn you that your mother has a limited capacity for empathy and compassion?"

"You did," I confirmed.

"Did I or did I not try to save you from the disappointment that inevitably goes with being the child of a self-absorbed supermodel?"

"You did. By lying through your teeth."

"Hey, an agent's gotta do what an agent's gotta do." She smiled as the world's hottest waiter approached the table, ordered quiche and black coffee, then tapped away at her Black-Berry while I ordered crepes and tried not to drool visibly in front of Gavin.

"No wonder you never get tired of this place," I marveled, watching him walk away. "That guy should be on the dessert menu."

"Don't be crude, pet." She tucked her BlackBerry back into her purse and snapped back into her no-nonsense routine. "And when the food comes, eat fast. I have a meeting in Century City in an hour."

"Then we'd better get down to business." I raised an eyebrow. "Tell me about Thomas."

She sighed. "The Thomas situation . . . it really is complicated."

I leaned closer. "Why?"

"Oh no, you don't. I'm not giving away any more details. All I'm going to say is this: I know your mother has failed you a lot over the last eighteen years, but she had a very good reason for standing you up last night. Here." Laurel reached into her jacket pocket and extracted an envelope with my name scrawled on it. "She left this for you."

"Mom did?" I ran my fingers over the thick white paper. "She left again?"

"For now," my aunt hedged. "And that's all you're getting out of me. This is between you and her."

"And Thomas," I added. "My . . . brother? Right? Come on, give me a hint."

She set her jaw. "I've said too much already. Back to business. How did the audition go last week?"

"The razor commercial?" I nibbled on my muffin. "I thought it went okay, but I take it they didn't call you and offer me the job."

"Nope. I might be able to get you in front of a casting director for a sitcom reading next week, but don't get your hopes up—you'll be competing against pretty seasoned vets. Like Bissy Billington to the tenth power."

I nodded. "I'm trying, Laurel. I really am."

"I know you are." She gave me a patronizing little pat on the hand. "But this is a very tough business. You're not going to get every job you go out for."

"Yeah, I've had five auditions since I booked the Samba commercial. Five! And I didn't get a single callback!"

She laughed. "Five auditions is nothing. You're just spoiled because you got hired the very first time you auditioned. The reality is, if you're talented and beautiful and very, very lucky, you'll book maybe five percent of the jobs you audition for."

"Five percent?!?"

"And that's being optimistic."

"But that means I have"—I did a quick series of calculations in my head—"fourteen auditions to go before my next job!"

"At least," she agreed. "And who knows? You might hit a dry spell for fifty, sixty tryouts. But you can skew the odds in your favor by networking and honing your craft. How are the acting classes going?"

"Uh . . ." Would that be the acting class I dropped out of? "Great. I'm thinking about switching to an improv group, though. To prep me for comedy."

"*You* want to do comedy?"

"Sure." I smiled winningly. "I can be funny."

"If you say so." Her face lit up as Gavin approached with her coffee. She grabbed the cup and threw back half of the steaming liquid in one gulp. "I'll have Harper scout out possible acting coaches and classes. Don't worry—I won't tell her it's for you."

"Thanks." If Harper had her way, I'd be enrolled in clown school—or worse, *mime* school—before you could say "seltzer-water vendetta."

"And I'll even help out with the networking. There's a magazine launch party tomorrow night; I can pull a few strings and get you in. Any interest?"

"Definitely. Can Coelle and Jacinda come, too?"

"I'll see what I can do." She winked. "And listen, speaking of Coelle . . . can I ask you something? Confidentially?"

I swallowed hard, my mouth suddenly dry. "Sure."

"Does Coelle seem, I don't know, *different* lately?"

"Different?" I tried to sound nonchalant. "Different how?"

"I can't put my finger on it," she mused, "but she's been acting weird. Like she's . . . she's . . ."

I remembered the euphoric expression on her face that morning as she kissed Quentin. "Happy?"

"Maybe that's it." She nodded.

"Why do you ask?"

"Well, her director says she's been very distracted on-set lately and when I met her for lunch last week, she actually ordered dessert." Laurel tucked an errant wave of hair behind her ear. "Happy. I guess that makes sense. I've never seen her like this."

"How long have you known her?" I asked.

"Oh, about five or six years."

"And you've never seen her happy?"

"Most child stars aren't happy, Eva. They're too busy for messy little details like emotions."

"Well, is it a problem that she's happy?"

"No; her mother's just worried that she's losing focus and I agree."

"I think she's gaining focus, not losing it," I bristled. "All she wants to do is turn eighteen, get the hell out of here, and go to college. Her main life goal is a veterinary degree, not an Oscar."

"Well, as her agent, my job is to get her the Oscar. She and her mom will have to battle out the rest. Just keep an eye on her, and let me know if she gets too . . ."

"Happy?" I said sarcastically. "I'm the fun police now? No joy on my watch?"

She gave me a piercing look. "I'm not being nosy, pet, but Coelle has a history—"

"The bulimia? I know. But that was, like, years ago. Why would you think she would start up—"

"Just let me know if she starts acting erratically, all right? And stop being such a truculent little mule about it."

"I'm not being truculent," I muttered, wishing I had one of Coelle's exhaustive vocab lists so I could check the definition.

"If only that were true. Now let's pretend we're a normal family and try to enjoy our breakfast, all right?"

"Hang on." I ripped open the envelope my mom had sent. "Let me read this first."

Baby girl—
You're probably mad that I didn't show yesterday, right? I tried to make it up to you by sending your boyfriend Davey. (I figured you'd rather see a cute guy than your lunatic mom any day of the week!) I didn't get to talk to him long, but he sounds really nice.
I know it seems like I'm running away again, but I'm doing the right thing. I have to make some changes. But I'm coming back soon. Just hang in there a little longer. You have to believe in me.
Love,
M.

"What?" Laurel winced as she studied my expression. "Is it bad?"

"It's fine," I said softly, folding the stationery into a fat little square. "Do you have any paper? I want to write her back."

"You do? Well, that's great! You guys are finally communicating!" Laurel rummaged through her briefcase and pulled out some stationery embossed with the Allora Agency logo. "I am so proud of you, Eva. This is a real step forward."

I smiled sweetly at her, then wrote:

Mom—
   1. I don't believe in you.
   2. His name is DANNY.
   3. We broke up.
   E.
P.S. ~~Bite me~~ ~~Go to~~ Don't send me any more letters.

"Here." I folded up the note and handed it to my aunt. "Make sure she gets this as soon as possible. And don't read it, okay? It's personal."

"See?" The next morning, while I washed the dishes in the sink with ferocious energy, Coelle sat at the kitchen table, reading my mother's letter. "She's sick! She's sick and twisted and if she thinks I'm going to put up with any more of her crap, she is sadly mistaken."

"She does sound a little unstable," Coelle agreed.

"I know! Running away is her answer to everything! And she doesn't even have the guts to face me—she always uses a letter or a phone call or my boyfriend to do her dirty work!"

"Danny's not your boyfriend anymore," Coelle pointed out helpfully.

I snatched back the letter, soaking it with my wet, soapy hands. The black ink bled into my fingers as I wadded up the page, crammed in into the garbage disposal, and flicked the switch next to the sink. The motor whirred to life, sending bits of paper flying up to the ceiling. *"That's* what she can do with her promises that next time will be different."

Coelle nodded. "Good for you."

"I'm mad as hell and I'm not gonna take it anymore!"

"Fight the power."

"She can take her secrets and her drama and shove it up her—"

"Listen, this probably isn't the best time to mention this, but you guys are in the G-Spot again."

"What? No!"

"Sorry. I didn't want to say anything, but I thought you should see it before we hit the *Trench* party tonight." *Trench* was the new magazine my aunt had mentioned. Coelle pulled an issue of *South of Sunset* out of her blue leather bag and handed it over without a word.

I flipped to the *Faces and Places* page, trying to steel myself for the latest installment of Gigi Geltin:

> Spies at my Valley outposts inform me
> that outmoded model Marisela Cordes

has given up on her Hollywood come-back and decamped to higher ground: Thousand Oaks, to be exact, where she was seen lunching and laughing with a man not her fidelity-challenged fiancé. Must be a nice change from all those slamming doors and wagging tongues.

I hear Mari's daughter, Eva, has picked up where Mom left off, pitching woo and dancing on tables all over the Westside. Look out, gents, Eva and her glam gal posse, Coelle Banerjee and Jacinda Crane-Laird, are due to hit the *Trench* party tonight at the Belmont. Talk about a triple threat!

"Okay, first of all, what the hell is 'pitching woo'?" I made a face. "It sounds obscene. Second of all, *how* does this newspaper keep track of my every move? The only way they could know all this is if Aunt Laurel told them, and she would never do that. Third of all: Thousand Oaks? Where's that?"

"About thirty minutes northwest of here. Off the one-oh-one freeway."

"But her letter reads like she went off to Timbuktu or Antarctica or something! I can't believe she ditched me to go scam some skeezebag in the eight-one-eight!"

"Don't worry about her." Coelle sounded determinedly

upbeat. "We're going to that magazine party and we're going to 'pitch woo' like nobody's business."

"Assuming that's legal."

"Even if it's not." She grinned. "Come on, let's go raid Jacinda's closet and decide what we're gonna wear tonight. Oh, and I told Quentin he could come along, okay? This is gonna be so fun!"

16

We all wore little black dresses to the *Trench* party: black chiffon for Jacinda, black lace for me, and black vinyl (I know!) for Coelle. Since Jacinda had appointed herself makeup artist, we all had on too much kohl liner and sparkly eye shadow, but as a trio, we made it work.

Then Quentin showed up. In a black suit with a pink shirt. And a shiny pink tie.

"What?" he asked when Jacinda opened the apartment door with a sneer. "Pink is in for guys. You have to be secure in your manhood to wear pink."

"I love it." Coelle rushed over to greet him, teetering on

the lethally high heels of her knee-high black vinyl boots *(I know!).* "You look great, honey."

"Thanks." He slung an arm around her and jerked his thumb toward the doorway. "We gotta get moving if we're going to hit the red carpet before the photogs split."

Photogs? I mouthed at Jacinda, who rolled her eyes, yanked up her strapless top, and said, "Come on, ladies. The three of us are going to knock 'em dead on the carpet."

"Yeah, about that." Coelle nibbled her bottom lip. "I was thinking that maybe I should work the carpet with Quentin. Seeing as we're a couple and all."

"But we're a triple threat," I reminded her. "Even Gigi Geltin agrees. United we kick ass, divided we don't."

"Yeah, we can do *Charlie's Angels* poses for the paparazzi," Jacinda added.

"But . . ." Coelle slipped her hand into Quentin's and ducked her head. "I promised Quentin."

Quentin jangled his car keys. "The soap opera rags'll only want pictures if we're together. That's the whole reason we're dating—to get some ink."

Coelle simpered up at him. "Well, that's not the *whole* reason we're dating."

"Oh. I know. Whatever, we're cool." He tugged her out to the courtyard. "See you guys there, okay? Meet you in the VIP lounge."

And with that, he hustled our roommate off to his new Porsche and his precious photo-op.

"That's it." Jacinda threw down her evening bag and stalked toward the kitchen. "Where's my meat cleaver?"

"Calm down." I grabbed her forearm. "The longer you spend looking for sharp, shiny instruments to dismember him, the later we're gonna be."

"Who cares? No party really starts till I get there, anyway. Oh, and that reminds me: *I* am not a member of your quote-unquote glam gal posse—*you* are a member of *mine*."

As usual, the red carpet was the psychological equivalent of a war zone—lots of shouting, shooting, and ruthless tactical strategies. All the photographers hollered at me to get out of the way so they could shoot Jacinda alone, and I happily obliged, leaving her to pose for a sea of flashbulbs while I headed inside the crowded nightclub to hunt down the girl who had spurned us in favor of Pink Shirt.

"Hi." Coelle had to yell directly into my ear in order to be heard over the deep pounding bass, clinking glass, and excited conversation in the VIP lounge. "Sorry about before—I shouldn't have ditched you guys for a boy. Forgive me, roomie, for I have sinned."

"That's okay." I took a few moments to check out the scene: disco balls, black leather booths, and red velvet walls. Lots of blonde, emaciated, actress types flirting with self-impressed power suits with gleaming white teeth and Botoxed foreheads. Everyone smiling widely as they glanced over each other's shoulders to make sure there was no one more important they could be talking to. The usual.

"What happened to Jacinda?" Coelle yelled.

"What do you think?" I grinned. "She's still posing for her adoring public."

"You okay?" she asked. "You look like you've been inhaling too much secondhand smoke or something."

I shook my head. "I'm fine. I just . . . I think I'm over the Hollywood party circuit. Everything is so plastic."

She nodded sympathetically. "You get jaded. Especially when you're single."

She had a point. If Danny and I were still together, I would have dragged him to this party with me. We could have holed up in one of the booths and laughed at all the self-impressed poseurs and pitched woo or whatever all night. But now . . .

"Hey. Wipe that lost kitty look off your face," Coelle warned. "Stop thinking about him. He kissed another girl. That's unforgivable, Eva. Look at the buffet of hot men here! You'll find somebody better. Somebody who'll treat you the way you deserve to be treated. Like Quentin treats me." She gazed dreamily over at her date, who was chatting up a redhead in a green dress, his eyes fixed firmly on her breasts.

"He's a prince, all right," I said.

"Ooh! Here we go." Coelle squinted into the crowd. "Right side of the bar. Two o'clock. Guy in a baseball cap checking you out."

I tried to see past all the Versace and Chanel. "What? Who?"

"Oh, wait." Coelle frowned. "Oh crap."

"What?" I craned my neck, desperately trying to pick out the guy she was talking about.

She grabbed my elbow and towed me halfway across the

room. "Don't look," she said through clenched teeth. "It's Danny."

My head whipped around. "Where?"

"Don't look!"

Too late. He was leaning against the tarnished zinc bartop, obscured by shadow and candlelight, but unmistakable.

He looked at me. I looked at him. The smoke and the music faded into the background, but neither of us made any move to approach the other.

And then the ho biscuit slithered up behind him and slid her arms around his waist.

"Oh my God," I breathed, instinctively lifting my hands to fix my hair and check my lipstick. "Did he see me? What is he *doing* here?"

"His dad is a producer and his stepmom is a big network casting director, right? He can get into any A-list event he wants." Coelle shook her head.

"Well, what is *she* doing here?" I stole another glance at the cleat chaser, who was stuffed into a tightly laced red leather corset.

"Just ignore them," Coelle advised. "Stop looking over there!"

"You guys said he only kissed her to make me jealous!" I cried. "You said there was no way he'd date her!"

"Eva." She placed her hands on my temples, forcing me to focus on her face. "Who cares? You're done. You're over him."

But I didn't feel very over him.

"All right, my public is finally satisfied. Now who wants a drink?" Jacinda strutted in, blocking my view of the bar. "I ordered you a kir royale—oof!" One of the Botox clones barged past her, slamming her into me. As she stumbled, her razor-sharp stiletto stabbed down on my bare toe.

"Ow!" I crashed back against a table full of drinks. Freezing cold liquid splashed all over my butt.

"Sorry." Jacinda steadied herself by grabbing my shoulder. "That unchivalrous jackass—"

"I forgive you," I squeaked. "Could you please get off my foot?"

"Right. Sorry." She yanked her spike heel out of my poor little foot. "Rough crowd tonight."

I peered down at the blood oozing out between my sandal straps. "Well, go get that guy's name and number, 'cause I'm suing him when they have to amputate my . . ." I trailed off as I looked back toward the bar.

"Eva? Hello?" Jacinda prompted. "Are we drinking or suing or what? Eva?"

I waved her away and limped across the room, wincing with every step. But I was too late—Danny was gone. And so was the cleat chaser.

The next week flew by in a flurry of auditions. Cars, cola, chips . . . I pitched them all with verve and panache. But I didn't book a single job. I didn't even get any callbacks.

"What are you whining about?" Jacinda demanded as we vroomed down Santa Monica Boulevard in her convertible. "You don't even want to do commercials—you're holding out for a movie or a J. J. Abrams series."

"No, that's you," I corrected. "*I'm* holding out for whatever I can get, the sooner, the better. I need money. And I need to get out of the Goose."

"Yes, yes, you do." She took a sharp right turn without even tapping the brakes. "That reminds me, could you stop parking that monstrosity outside the apartment building? It's humiliating the entire neighborhood."

"Where else am I supposed to park it?"

"The bottom of the ocean?" she suggested. "At the airport with the keys in the ignition, the windows open, and the engine running?"

"Someday you, too, are going to have to drive a crappy car," I vowed.

"I already do." She ran a stale yellow light, kissing her fingers and lifting them to the roof of the car near the rearview mirror. "This Benz is almost three years old."

"Oh, the humanity." I caressed the buttery, soft gray leather upholstery.

"I know. I die a thousand deaths every time I pull up to Geoffrey's or the Roosevelt Hotel. My parents say driving the passé mobile will build character, but I told them that they were a day late and a dollar short on that one." She slowed down long enough to wave and wink at the LAPD squad car next to us, then sped up again. "But listen. I have to talk to you about something. Valentine's Day is this weekend, right?"

"Not if you're single and bitter."

"Okay, well, I want Quentin to do something wildly romantic for Coelle. To show her that he really cares about her."

"But he *doesn't* really care about her."

"I don't want her to know that! I want her to feel special, cherished, all those girly Valentine's Day emotions."

"Why? So you can feel less guilty about what you did?"

"Well. Yeah." Jacinda cleared her throat. "Besides, she's been having a tough time on the show lately and—"

"Really?" I asked, surprised. Coelle always behaved so professionally on-set, I couldn't imagine anyone having a problem with her. "What's going on?"

"I don't know all the details; I guess the writers want her character to go off on some really weird plot twists at the end of the season, so she asked Laurel to talk some sense into them. But anyway, my point is, she's having enough trouble without Sir Wank-a-doo forgetting Valentine's Day. So here's what I'm thinking: I'll call him up—"

"Who? Quentin?"

"Yeah. And help him come up with a plan. Like, I'll mention that her favorite flower is freesia and her favorite restaurant is Cafe Del Rey and she prefers rubies to diamonds . . ." She trailed off as she noticed my expression. "What?"

"Jacinda. Come on."

She slammed on the brake, bringing the car to a screeching halt around the corner from our apartment. "Ooh, maybe I'll tell him to buy her a kitten! A white, fluffy one with a red bow around its neck. Better yet, a ruby-studded collar!"

"They've been a couple for, like, two weeks." I grabbed the door handle and closed my eyes as she threw the car into reverse and tried to parallel park in a space the size of a shoe box. "It's a little early for precious gems, don't you think?"

"No such thing. If he really likes her . . ." She folded her arms on the steering wheel and whomped her forehead down on her wrists. "He doesn't, though. He never has, he never will, and the guilt! The guilt! I'm going to hell, Eva!"

"And you think a furry kitten with a ruby collar will make you feel better?" I asked.

"I think it'll make Coelle feel better."

"A cat is not going to compensate for the fact that her boyfriend doesn't love her," I decreed. "Take it from someone who got a Wheaten terrier instead of a mom."

Jacinda rolled her head to peek at me with one eye. "Seriously?"

"Yep. My grandparents bought him for me when my mom dropped me off at their house for a 'weekend visit' and never came back. His name was Murphy and he was a great dog. But it's not like he made me forget that my mom had decided she'd rather carouse on yachts in Capri than teach me the alphabet."

"That is so messed-up."

"Plus, cats shed, you know. So unless you want long, white hairs all over your black Gucci—"

"Well? What else am I supposed to do?" She pounded the steering wheel, oblivious to the increasingly long line of traffic backing up behind us. "I can't make him love her, but I can make him buy her stuff."

"Jacinda, you sleeping with him has nothing to do with him not loving her. If it hadn't been you, it would've been someone else. You said it yourself: he's a soulless pretty boy. So if you're not going to tell her what you did—"

"I'm not."

"—then just stay out of it and let the relationship die of natural causes. Coelle's too smart to put up with his crap for long. If he doesn't do anything special for Valentine's Day, she'll see him for the toolio he truly is."

"You say that now." Jacinda rolled down her window to flip off the driver of the station wagon honking behind us. "But girls do stupid things when they're in love."

My mind flashed to a half-naked image of Danny Bristow. "You got that straight."

"Hey. Where were you guys?"

Coelle was already camped out in the living room when Jacinda and I walked through the door. Usually she worked all day during the week, but today she had nestled into the couch with a blue cashmere blanket, a bottle of iced tea, the remote, and . . . a big bowl of spaghetti.

"Oh my God." Jacinda pretended to faint. "Am I hallucinating or are you actually eating pasta?" She did a double take. "With Parmesan cheese?"

"Yeah, it was in the fridge so I threw it in the microwave." She didn't look away from the TV screen, which was showing an episode of *Animal Precinct* that I knew she'd already seen. (I knew this because she'd made both Jacinda and I sit through it when we'd wanted to watch *America's Next Top Model* instead.) "Sorry if you were planning to have it for dinner."

"That's okay," I said, trying not to stare as she forked up another huge bite of processed white flour and canned tomato sauce. "It's kind of old, though—does it taste okay?"

"Mm-hmm." She sighed deeply, turned up the volume, and curled into a tight little ball.

Jacinda and I exchanged a look. "Did something happen?" Jacinda asked. "With Quentin?"

Coelle frowned. "No. Of course not. Why would you say that?"

"Well, you're home instead of at work and you kind of look . . . um . . ."

Coelle's eyes were cold and flat. "How? How do I look?"

"You look good," Jacinda lied. "But, I mean, you're sitting there in pajamas and a blanket, eating actual food instead of bean sprouts and organic soy milk—"

"It's none of your business what I eat," Coelle snapped.

Jacinda tried for an appeasing smile. "Okay. But as long as you're on a roll here, wanna go get some french fries?"

"No. Just leave me alone."

I perched on the overstuffed arm of the sofa. "What happened today?"

"Nothing!" She pulled the top of the blanket over her head like a hood.

"Then why—"

"I'm fine." She got up, yanked the edge of the blanket out from under me, marched up to her room, and slammed the door with enough force to rattle the empty cans in the recycling bin.

Jacinda and I looked at each other, then at the empty bowl stained with pasta sauce sitting on the coffee table.

"Jeez," Jacinda said. "Maybe it's her mom?"

"Maybe it's the SAT?" I suggested.

"Maybe it's the full moon?"

As I slid down onto the couch cushion she'd vacated, something dug into my back. "Yowch." I leaned forward and pulled out an empty soda can. And a crumpled candy bar wrapper.

"Oh shit." Jacinda sprinted over and wrestled the candy bar wrapper away from me. "She's doing it again."

"What?" I asked.

"The whole bulimia thing."

"It's a candy bar wrapper and some noodles," I pointed out. "That doesn't mean anything. I mean, she could just be hungry, right?"

Jacinda shook her head. "The day before she started treatment last time, I found like six candy bar wrappers in the trash."

"But she did get help, right? Didn't they cure her?"

"Do I look like a psychiatrist to you? How do I know if they cured her? All I'm saying is, she's bingeing again. I just hope she's not—"

Two more door slams upstairs, a long pause, and then a flushing toilet.

"Son of a bitch." Jacinda slammed her car keys down on the table. "She's throwing up."

"Not necessarily," I cautioned. "Don't jump to conclusions."

She gave me a withering look. "You are so stupid."

"Maybe she just had to pee!" I argued.

"Or maybe she's shoving her finger down her throat." Her face was grim. "Don't start with me, Snow White. I know I'm right."

•   •   •

Later that evening, the aparment's landline rang, and when I picked it up a perky female voice asked for Coelle.

"Hang on." I ran up the stairs, rapped softly on her bedroom door, and waited.

No response.

I knocked again. "Coelle?"

Nothing.

So I hurried back down to inform the caller that my roommate was, to use Jacinda terminology, "indisposed."

"She's sleeping," I explained.

"Oh, okay. Well, this is Georgia Martinez. I'm the assistant director on *Twilight's Tempest* and I'm just calling to make sure she's feeling better."

I frowned. "She, uh . . . she seems okay."

"Great. After she passed out on-set today, we were all a little worried."

I glanced toward the couch where Coelle had spent the afternoon. "Yeah, we're kind of freaked out ourselves."

"So she went to a doctor?" Georgia pressed. "I know she said it was just an electrolyte imbalance, but we like to be on the safe side. Especially since that's the second time this week."

17

Danny called on Valentine's Day. I stared at my cellphone, trying to decide whether I should answer. After four rings' worth of panicked indecision, the call went to voicemail.

I managed to wait about ten more seconds before checking my messages, and sure enough, there he was: "Hi. It's Danny. I, uh . . . I . . . call me back, okay?"

The sound of his voice was like a shot of warm and fuzzy straight to the heart. I glanced around furtively, making sure Coelle and Jacinda weren't around to witness my moment of weakness, and called him back.

He picked up immediately. "Hello?"

I tried to sound nonchalant. "You called?"

"I just left you a voicemail. Why didn't you answer your phone?" He sounded very far away; I wasn't sure if it was a bad wireless connection or a bad, you know, emotional one.

"I couldn't decide whether to answer or not and by the time I made up my mind, you'd hung up."

"Oh."

I waited for him to keep going. When he didn't, I asked, "So what's up?"

"Well. Here's the thing. I wanted to explain about the magazine party last week."

"Oh." My voice went up about two octaves. "That."

"I know it looked bad—"

"That you showed up at the bar with your new girlfriend all over you like a nasty, peeling sunburn and then ran away like a baseball cap-wearing version of Cinderella as soon as you saw me? Yeah, it did look pretty bad."

"I get why you're mad, but—"

"Listen. I don't want to see you guys making out at every press event I go to. We have to set some ground rules." I paused. "Since when do you even like going to Hollywood parties? I thought you said they were insipid and soul-numbing. Or has your girlfriend changed your mind? Does she have a name, by the way?"

"Tylee," he muttered. "And she's not my girlfriend."

"Oh, my mistake. Your fuck buddy."

"Would you knock it off?" He started to sound really annoyed. Good. "She's not any of those things."

"Really." I turned up the snottiness. "Then what is she, pray tell?"

He mumbled something I couldn't make out.

"What's that?"

He sighed. "She's kind of my stalker."

"You can do better than *that*."

"No, seriously. I mean it."

"So do I. I'm not an idiot! I saw you kiss her on the baseball field. She didn't exactly ambush you with a Taser and handcuffs!"

"Okay, yeah, I did kiss her," he admitted. "She's always hanging around with different guys from the team, and I knew you were waiting to talk to me and I wanted to . . ." I could practically hear him turning red over the phone. "That was immature and stupid, I admit it."

"Well, at least we agree on that."

"But that was it! One kiss! The end! I shouldn't have kissed her and if I could take it back, I would, but I swear that's all it was. I swear."

"Then why did you bring her to the *Trench* party?"

"I didn't!" He sounded so worked up that I was beginning to believe him. "She called my roommate, found out where I was going, and followed me! Ever since I kissed her that day, she's been texting me, showing up at my classes, coming to all my practices."

"Well, she thinks you like her," I pointed out. "Seeing as you kissed her and all."

"No—there is no 'and all.' I explained to her that I wasn't

interested and 'it's not you, it's me' like a *hundred* times. She won't give up!"

"Then maybe you should give her a chance," I purred. "I'm sure she's better than me in bed, anyway."

"Damn it, Eva! I went to the *Trench* party for you. I knew you'd be there and I wanted to see you."

I finally stopped baiting him. "But how did you know . . . ?"

"The G-Spot. It said you and your roommates were going to be there."

I blinked. "So while Tylee was stalking you, you were stalking me?"

"I wasn't *stalking* you. I don't call you every hour, on the hour, and use psychological torture to get your roommate to tell me where you are."

"Psychological torture?"

"She showed up at our room and blasted *The Little Mermaid* soundtrack until he cracked."

I started to laugh. "You're making this up."

"I wish I was."

It felt so good to laugh with him again. I ached from missing him.

"Listen," he said. "I'm sorry. You trusted me and I blew it. I know I can never make that up to you."

I surprised myself by saying, "Maybe you can." I wanted to try a fresh start.

But that meant he had to know the truth, the whole truth, and nothing but the truth.

"What are you saying, Eva?"

I took a deep breath. "I miss you. I need to talk to you. Face-to-face. About everything."

The ensuing pause was so long, I thought he might have hung up on me. "Danny?"

"I'm here. I miss you, too."

"But I have something I need to tell you. Before we, you know . . ."

"A deep, dark secret?" he teased.

"Kind of. So listen, when can we get together? Do you have any time tomorrow?"

"I have to train all day tomorrow."

"The whole day?"

"Yeah. Remember I said some scouts might be checking out our early games? Well, I might have the chance to try out for the national team."

"Like the major leagues?"

"Like the Olympics. The junior team. We'll see. But what about Monday? My afternoon's wide open."

"I have an audition at three-thirty, but I should be home by five."

"I'll pick you up Monday at five."

"Okay. And, hey, that's really great news about the Olympics. God. That's a huge deal."

"Nothing's happened yet," he cautioned.

"It will," I said. "Everyone needs southpaw pitchers, right?"

He started to laugh. "Look who's been brushing up on her baseball terminology."

"I'm a baseball goddess," I assured him. "I can spit and grab my crotch with the best of them. And you should hear me go off about the designated hitter rule."

"I can't wait. And Eva?"

"Yeah?"

"Happy Valentine's Day."

After Jacinda and I confronted Coelle about passing out on-set (Coelle, of course, chalked it all up to everybody's favorite celebrity excuse: "exhaustion," at which point Jacinda gave her a hard look and said, "You're not *pregnant,* are you?"), we decided that she could not be trusted on her own and tried to arrange our schedules so that one of us would be home with her for the rest of the weekend. Just to keep an eye on her. And the candy bars. And the toilet.

But despite the fact that Coelle spent all of Valentine's Day parked in front of the TV—no flowers, no rubies, not even a phone call from Quentin—she didn't seem angry or depressed. She just seemed kind of hollow. Like the hotel lights were still on, but the guest had checked out. And I didn't find any more evidence of pigging out and throwing up; I barely saw her eat at all.

"Don't let that fool you," Jacinda railed on Sunday night when I mentioned this to her. "This is the calm before the storm."

"But I've been with her all day and she's had a bowl of Kashi and a mango. That's it."

"Yeah, until you go to bed. Don't be so naïve. Bulimics are masters of deception."

"'Masters of deception'?" I repeated, thinking about Coelle's calm, forthright confidence.

"Hey. Who's watched her disintegrate into a quivering mass of imbalanced electrolytes before, you or me?"

"It's just hard to believe that Coelle . . . I mean, she always has so much sense and self-control."

"Exactly. Eating disorders are all about control," Jacinda informed me with the expertise born from years of attending boarding school with high-society princesses who grew up chanting the mantra, You can never be too rich or too thin. "That's how I know something big is up with her. If everything were hunky-dory, she wouldn't be scarfing carbs and then praying to the porcelain god."

I stared at her. "Did you just say 'hunky-dory'?"

"Yeah. I must have picked it up from you. Next thing you know I'll be respecting my elders and taking a vow of eternal celibacy." She shuddered.

"Well, all I know is that I've been watching her all day, and she seems totally back to normal."

"Until you go to bed," Jacinda corrected.

"Whatever. I checked the fridge last night and all the cupboards, and there's nothing incriminating in there."

"Like she's really going to keep her stash in plain sight. She's probably got it hidden away in the back of her closet."

"Then how am I supposed to find—"

"Did you check the bottom of the trash bag?"

I glanced over at the blue plastic trash can by the dishwasher. "No."

"Well, you have to start digging if you want to find anything. In our trash and in the Dumpster behind the building."

"Jacinda, get real. I'm not going Dumpster diving just to bust—"

"She's too smart to leave the evidence where you can find it! If she were on drugs, do you think she'd shoot up right in front of you?"

"Of course not. But—"

"Food is her drug!" Jacinda's green eyes blazed with intensity. "And she's using again! I know it!"

"Well, what should we do?" I was getting pretty intense myself.

"Abduct her while she's sleeping, tie her up, and haul her off to a therapist?"

"Hmm." Jacinda nodded, giving this option serious consideration. "That's not a bad idea."

"We can't keep her under surveillance forever," I pointed out. "I have an audition tomorrow, and you have to . . . do whatever it is you do all day."

"Personal trainer in the morning, mani/pedi at noon, screen test in the afternoon."

I rolled my eyes. "You forgot shopping."

"I'll shop online at the salon while they're working on my toes."

"Well, we have to tell someone." I thought this over for a minute. "Her mother?"

"God, no. Coelle will never forgive us if we drag her mom into this."

"Then it'll have to be Laurel," I decided. "I wonder if the *Twilight's Tempest* people already called her."

"Well, either way, we've got to—"

We both jumped as we heard Coelle's bedroom door open, then her footsteps on the stairs.

"Hey, guys." She was wearing the same gray yoga pants and faded red T-shirt she'd had on all weekend. Between her newly pallid skin tone and the deep purple circles under her eyes, she looked positively gaunt. "What's going on?"

"Nothing." I glanced guiltily at Jacinda, who managed to maintain an air of detached indifference. "Nothing at all. Why, what's going on with you?"

"Just finished an essay on *Walden* for my tutor. I have to be on set superearly, so I'm going to bed."

"What time are you going to be home tomorrow?"

"Maybe four or four-thirty. Why?"

"Because Danny's coming over at five and I have an audition and I want to be sure someone'll be here to let him in."

Both my roommates practically gave themselves whiplash in their haste to get the dirt.

"Danny returns? Is he finally going to finish what he started with you?" Jacinda licked her lips, all lascivious.

"You're going to get back together with him after he rubbed that groupie right in your face?" Coelle shook her head.

"Ease up, both of you." I crossed my arms. "We are just going to talk."

"Wear my black leather skirt and you won't need to do any talking," Jacinda said.

"Take him back and I'll never respect you again," Coelle added.

"My relationship is my business," I said firmly. "So just let him in when he comes by and keep the commentary to yourself."

Jacinda turned to Coelle. "Jeez, what a dictator."

"I know. After all we've done for her."

"Taken her under our wing."

"Treated her like one of our own."

"And this is the thanks we get."

I fought my way back into the conversation. "Shut it, both of you. I don't tell *you* what to do with *your* boyfriends."

"My boyfriend wouldn't kiss some girl he doesn't even know to get back at me for not putting out," Coelle huffed.

I saw my opening and made my move. "So everything's still good with Quentin?"

She hesitated ever so slightly before replying, "Of course. We're really happy."

"Great."

"Why would you even ask that?"

"Because . . . nothing."

"No, really. What are you trying to say?"

I hoped Jacinda might jump in to help me answer this, but she had apparently gone blind, deaf, and mute.

I shrugged. "We—excuse me, *I*—noticed you seem a little stressed lately."

"Stressed?" She put her hands on the hips of the baggy pants she'd been wearing for three days straight. "I'm not stressed!"

"And then you didn't go out with Quentin for Valentine's Day, so I thought maybe—"

"He had to fly out to New Mexico to work last weekend."

"He did?"

"Yeah. But before he left, he gave me the sweetest card—he wrote me a poem and everything—for Valentine's Day. Paranoid much?"

Five pairs of Gucci slingbacks says he downloaded the poem from, like, www.PlagiarizedGenericSchmaltz.com. "Oh. Well, that's sweet."

She stared at me. "What? You think he should have sent flowers?"

"No!"

"You think he should have spent a lot of money on some extravagant gift?" Her eyes welled up. "Valentine's Day is just a meaningless commercial holiday, okay? He doesn't have to shower me with roses just because the calendar says he should. I don't need a bunch of material trinkets to know that Quentin cares about me. That poem he wrote is worth more to me than all the diamonds in Cartier."

Jacinda emitted a strangled cough.

"You're jealous, aren't you?" Coelle glared at me. "Well, stay out of my life. Don't try to poison my relationship just because Quentin loves me more than Danny ever loved you."

"Is he here yet?" I burst through the apartment door at 5:30 on Monday, breathless and sweaty from my four-block dash from the only available parking spot big enough to accommodate the Goose. "My audition ran long, and then traffic was horrible, and—"

"Cool your jets; he's not here." Jacinda looked up from her copy of *Us Weekly.* "Good thing, too—you look like you've been lifting weights in a sauna. Go hose yourself down."

"He's not?" I checked the kitchen clock. "But he was supposed to be here half an hour ago. Are you sure?"

"Very sure." She flipped a page and studied a photo spread of the *Trench* party, presumably hoping to spot herself. "I think I remember the last thirty minutes pretty well."

"Well . . ." I dropped my purse on the hall table and peeled off the heavy wool cardigan that served as the Los Angeles version of a parka. "Maybe Coelle answered the door?"

She shook her head without looking up from her magazine. "Coelle's still at work."

"And he didn't call?"

"Eva." She tapped one fingernail on the table.

"Sorry, I know you'd tell me, but . . ." I pushed my hair back from my face and racked my brains. Where could he be? Maybe baseball practice had run long. Maybe he got stuck in traffic. Maybe Tylee had him chained to her bed.

Jacinda clicked her tongue. "No offense, but Danny's not really turning out to be the world's most reliable guy, is he?"

"That's the thing, though—he *is.* You were right about him being a thirty-five-year-old accountant. If he says he's gonna be somewhere, he is." I blanched as the worst-case scenario occurred. "Oh my God. What if he's dead?"

"Shut up. He's not dead."

"What if he is?"

"What if you've lost your crazy-ass mind?" She scowled

down at an interview with one of her more notorious exes. "He's still alive, he's still boring as hell, and he'll knock on the door any second now."

But he didn't. I waited thirty minutes, then another thirty, before accepting the fact that he wasn't coming.

I grabbed my cellphone and my keys, then headed out to the one place in West Hollywood where I could talk in total privacy—the Goose.

18

"Hello?" Danny picked up on the third ring and he didn't sound happy to hear my voice.

"Hey. What happened to you?" I propped my knee against the backseat of the Goose. "I thought you were picking me up at five."

"You weren't there at five," he pointed out. "Only Jacinda was."

"Yeah, but . . ." Wait. How did he know Jacinda had been in the apartment? She said he hadn't come by. "My audition ran long." I forced a laugh. "But aren't I worth waiting for?"

"I have to go." His voice sounded cold.

"Hey. I thought we were going to talk?"

"There's nothing to talk about."

"Danny! Why are you being like this?"

"I know about you and Jeff."

I inhaled sharply. "How did you find out about that?"

His laugh was bitter. "Yeah, I didn't think you'd deny it."

"Did Jacinda tell you? She did, didn't she?"

"It doesn't matter who told me."

"Listen, let me explain—"

"Don't."

"No, really, you have to hear me out." I curled into a tight little ball. "I was upset, we had just had that big fight—"

"I cannot believe you gave me so much crap about kissing Tylee when you *slept* with someone else." He still sounded cold, but also furious. "You had sex with Jeff! That's like . . . like I gave you a paper cut and you retaliated by dropping a nuclear bomb. You're such a hypocrite. And a liar."

"I was going to tell you," I swore. "Today!"

"You had plenty of chances to tell me," he pointed out, "and you didn't. You let me take all the blame for everything while you lied and lied and lied."

I dug my fingernails into the palm of my hand. "I know. I should have told you. I wanted to. But I just . . ."

"What?"

"I was afraid you'd react the way you're reacting right now."

"I knew you had something going on with Jeff! I knew it!"

"No, I didn't!" I cried. "But after you and I had that fight at the Somerset, I was so hurt and confused—"

"That you accidentally took off all your clothes and hopped into bed?"

"It wasn't like that, Danny! You have to believe me."

"No, actually, I don't. You want Jeff so bad, you can have him."

"I only want you! And I—" Part of me wanted to tell him that, although I had gotten naked with Jeff, I hadn't actually had sex with him. The rest of me argued that this was not a great idea. The physical technicalities didn't change the fact that I'd *intended* to go all the way. "I'm sorry," I finished lamely. "The whole thing with Jeff was, well, it was unforgivable."

When he didn't say anything, I plowed ahead with, "But I hope you'll try to forgive me anyway. Because I meant what I said at the Grove. I love you."

Dead silence. Never a good sign.

"Danny? Hello? At least talk to me."

"I'm leaving."

"What? Don't hang up!"

"No, I mean I'm leaving town. I'm going to the national team trials in Florida."

"That's amazing! Are you excited?"

"I'm not talking to you about this." He definitely didn't sound excited. "You're a distraction. I have to focus on baseball and my future. Not you. I have a seven A.M. flight to Orlando on Wednesday for a tryout that could change my life. And I'm not going to let you and Jeff ruin it for me."

"There is no 'me and Jeff'!" I protested.

"That's it. I'm hanging up."

"Wait!" I pressed the phone against my ear so hard I'd probably have a permanent impression in the side of my head. "What airline are you flying?"

"Continental." Then suspicion crept into his voice. "Why?"

"Because maybe I could meet you at LAX for breakfast and we could—"

"No way. Not interested."

"But—"

"Get it through your head, Eva: I don't want to see you. So don't call me anymore. Don't e-mail me, don't drop by. Leave me alone. I mean it." This time he really did hang up.

I grabbed a pen out of my purse and scribbled down "Continental, 7 A.M., LAX" on the back of my hand.

Then I slammed out of the Goose and headed inside to have it out with Jacinda.

"You told him!" I slammed the front door behind me, stalked over to the kitchen table, and got right in her face. "You bitch!"

Jacinda didn't even stir. She remained curled up in her chair, poring over the Fashion Police section of *Us*. "Okay, everyone knows I'm a bitch. So there's no point in getting all worked up about it now. But after that, I'm lost. I told who what?"

"You told Danny that I had sex with Jeff! Which was A, a lie, and B, a total violation of our pact."

"Our pact?" She closed the magazine, smirking. "The famed Cordes–Crane-Laird Peace Accord of 2006?"

"Why would you tell him?" I jabbed my index finger into her arm. "What is wrong with you?"

"Ow. Get your grubby paws off me before I have you arrested for assault." She brushed off her shirt, straightening the wrinkles I'd left in the pale blue silk. "If you must know, I didn't tell Danny anything."

"Well, if you didn't tell him, how did he find out?"

Her eyes widened. "He found out? Ooh, you're in trouble."

"No kidding! Haven't you been listening to a word I've said?"

"Eh. Fifty percent."

"You promised you wouldn't tell! You looked me right in the eye and gave me your word—"

"Oh my God, keep your G-string on. I said I didn't tell him, and I meant it."

"You *also* said he didn't come by this afternoon," I pointed out.

"He didn't."

"Well, then how did he know that you were home and I wasn't?"

"I don't know! And anyway, why would I tell him anything?"

"Because you're mean? Because you're bored? Because you get off on other people's suffering?"

Her nostrils flared as she picked up the magazine, then slammed it back down on the table. *"I didn't tell him."*

"Yes, you did! You broke your promise! So guess what? I'm telling Coelle about you and Quentin!"

"You wouldn't!"

"Watch me." I snatched up my cell, scrolled through the address book, and clicked on Coelle's number. "I'm calling her right now."

Jacinda launched herself over the table with incredible gymnastic speed and agility, tackled me, and sent my cellphone flying into the TV screen.

We tumbled over the back of the sofa, clawing and thrashing and kicking.

"Call her and die!" Jacinda yowled.

I blocked her attempt at a right hook. For a girl who grew up on Park Avenue, she was quite the street fighter.

She grabbed a handful of hair and yanked. "Don't make me scar you for life!"

"I'm telling her!" I threw her off balance with a perfectly timed elbow jab and shoved her face into a cushion. "She deserves to know that you slept with her precious boyfriend!"

"When?" came a soft voice from across the room.

Both of us froze in place, panting heavily.

"When did you sleep with Quentin?"

I released my death grip on Jacinda's neck as soon as she stopped trying to maul me, and she lifted her head from the depths of the sofa.

"Tell me that's not Coelle," she whispered.

"It is." The voice was a lot louder this time. "And I want some answers."

"What are you doing here?" Jacinda sputtered, flopping back over the sofa. "I thought you were at work."

"Nope." Coelle stood on the bottom step of the carpeted

198 BETH KILLIAN

stairway, staring at us. She was *still* wearing the gray yoga pants and red shirt she'd had on all weekend.

"You've been in the apartment this whole time?" I clarified.

"Yep." Her unblinking stare was getting a little unnerving.

"You said you had to be on set today!" Jacinda insisted, as if this would somehow make everything okay. "You said you had an early call."

"Yeah, well, that was a lie." Coelle slumped back against the wall, her head pitching forward. "I'm not even allowed on the *Twilight's Tempest* set anymore. I got fired."

"When?" Jacinda and I chorused.

"Last week. The writers and the producers decided that they wanted my character to start having sex and doing drugs and robbing banks and I'm not twenty-one."

"What does being twenty-one have to do with anything?" I piped up.

"They didn't want an underage actor portraying 'adult' events. Some moral clause or legal thing or whatever. So they gave me the boot and hired a new actress to take my place."

"They didn't even kill your character off?"

"Nope. Just found some brunette chick with big boobs and the right birthdate. In a few weeks, there'll be a new Hester Higgenbotham on the show and everyone will forget all about me."

"But then . . ." I struggled to make sense of her schedule. "Where have you been all day?"

"Were you ever planning to tell us?" Jacinda huffed.

"I'm telling you now," she pointed out. "And now you can tell me all about you and Quentin."

"I have no idea what you're talking about," Jacinda insisted.

Coelle turned to me. "Eva?"

"Um, what she said," I hedged.

Coelle returned her focus to Jacinda. "How many times did you do him?"

Jacinda gave up denying and moved on to begging. "It was before I knew you liked him, hand to God."

"How many times?"

"Once. Okay, twice. Okay, three times. And it wasn't even that good. I'm sure he was thinking of you the whole time."

Coelle nodded, her expression oddly serene. "Did he spend Valentine's Day with you?"

"Of course not." Jacinda frowned. "Hey. I thought you said he was in New Mexico."

"Who knows where he was? He was probably off sleeping with some other girl. The *new* Hester Higgenbotham."

"No, Coelle, I'm sure—"

"I haven't heard from him since I got fired. He won't even answer my calls. Now that I can't get him into premiere parties or *Soap Opera Digest*, it's like I never existed." She turned to address the wall instead of me. "You were right, okay? Are you happy? He was just using me for sex and publicity and . . . Jacinda . . . and . . ." She covered her face with her hands as her voice broke into bare, heaving sobs. "I actually believed that there might be one decent guy in the world who would prefer me to you. I'm such an idiot!"

"No, you're not," Jacinda countered. "*He* is. Sure, I'm blonde and flashy and sophisticated, but honestly? If I were looking for a girlfriend, I'd rather date you than me."

"Me, too," I agreed, which earned me a filthy look from Jacinda.

"What am I going to do?" Coelle collapsed in a heap on the ratty tan carpet. "I loved him. I really did. And I thought he loved me, too."

Jacinda ripped a paper towel off the roll on the counter and wordlessly passed it over. Coelle blew her nose and kept ranting. "What am I gonna do now? Fired, rejected, cheated on . . ."

"He will pay for his crimes," Jacinda promised. "Trust me. I know people . . ."

"This is your chance!" I exclaimed. "You always said you hated doing that show. Well, now you're free. You can do what you've always wanted—go to college and start a normal life. All that studying for the SAT is finally gonna pay off."

This just made her cry harder.

It was frightening to see her so vulnerable and out of control; she'd always been so above it all.

"I don't know how to live a normal life," she choked out. "I don't fit in; I don't make friends. You can't study for real life like you can for the SAT."

"I'll help you," I offered. "I had the most normal, suburban life of all time."

"Child, please. You're a freak," Jacinda scoffed.

Coelle ignored us. "Acting is all I know how to do. I hate it sometimes, but it's who I am. If I'm a failure at that, how am I going to succeed at anything else? I tried to be in a normal relationship like a normal girl and look how that turned out. *Failure.*"

Still sniffling, she slunk upstairs and shut her bedroom door. Jacinda and I crept up after her and held our breath, listening. Sure enough, we heard the telltale crinkle of cellophane from inside her room.

"I've never seen her like this," I whispered when we got back to the kitchen.

"I have." She shook her head sadly. "Once. It didn't end well."

"Look." I put my hands on my hips and made my stand. "Bulimia is serious. She needs help, and she needs it now. There's only one thing left to do."

"Hunt down Quentin and stick his head on a pike outside Sleeping Beauty's castle at Disneyland?"

"Tell Laurel." I grabbed my car keys. "I'm going to the agency right now."

"Hi there, Eva." Bissy Billington ambushed me as I headed across the courtyard. As always, she was wearing her signature color: white sweater, white skirt, pearl earrings. Ugh.

"Hi." I stared straight ahead, determined not to engage.

"Bad day?" She oozed fake sympathy.

"You could say that."

"Fight with your boyfriend?" she cooed. "That's a cryin' shame."

"Yeah. Thanks for caring." I made it all the way to the sidewalk. Then it hit me. "Wait a minute." I marched back toward her. "How did you know I had a fight with Danny?"

"Well, he seemed pretty mad after he dropped by this afternoon." She paused, her blue eyes shining. "Almost as if someone told him that his girlfriend was sleepin' around."

I gasped. "You."

"Almost as if someone had been sittin' in the courtyard two weeks ago and seen you let some scruffy blond guy into your apartment in the middle of the night. And then seen him running out the door an hour later. Half-naked."

I waved my car key at her like a weapon. "*You*! You and C Money!"

"Guess I just slipped up when I saw Danny today." She scrunched up her nose when she smiled. "Oopsie! He got all fired up, but I told him you probably had a perfectly reasonable explanation. Right?"

"How petty can you get?" I stalked toward her, my fists clenched. "You've ruined everything, you little—"

"Aw, sugar plum, he dumped you? Too bad." She turned on her heel and sashayed back toward her apartment. "He seemed like a real nice boy."

"You'll pay for this," I yelled after her, shaking my pile of mail in the air. "And C Money, too! I"ll . . . I'll . . . damn it, you'll pay!"

She minced up the stairs to her apartment's door, throwing me a smug little smile from the top step. "I tried to warn you, darlin'. Don't mess with Texas."

19

Even though it was well after five o'clock, I knew Laurel usually worked late. Way late. She wasn't answering either her office or cellphone, so I took a chance and drove straight to the agency. I finally caught a break when I entered the Allora lobby: Harper wasn't there. The huge chrome clock on the wall read 7:15—she'd probably gone home for the night (or down to the storage room to sharpen her horns and devour slabs of raw meat).

I headed down the long white corridor, listening for any sounds of life, until I reached the grand double doors at the end. Not wanting to barge in on another meeting of the Hair Gel Brigade, I cleared my throat and knocked softly.

"Hello?" I called. "Aunt Laurel? Can I talk to you for a sec?"

No response. I peeked in, but the room was empty.

So I crossed the hall to her office, repeated the knocking and the throat clearing, and this time, I got a muffled reply.

"Oh good, you're here." I placed my hand on the doorknob. "Can I come in?"

She yelled something—I couldn't decipher what—but she sounded enthusiastic, so I opened the door and stepped into her office.

The first thing I saw was the broad, musclebound back of a shirtless guy. The next thing I saw was my aunt's face peeking over his shoulder.

Her face was pink. Her hair was mussed. Her suit was crumpled up on the floor.

"Eva?" she shrieked.

I clapped my hands over my mouth.

"What are you doing here?" she gasped, clutching the guy closer to cover her chest. Her legs dangled over the desk, still in stockings and high heels. The guy twisted around to look at me, at which point I caught a glimpse of Laurel's black garter belt.

I moved my hands from my mouth to my eyes and started backing out to the hall. "Sorry, I didn't . . ."

And then I parted my fingers to take another look at the shirtless guy's face. *"Gavin?"*

The waiter from Sojo frowned. "Have we met?"

"Of course you've met," Laurel hissed at him. "She was at breakfast with me the other day."

"Well, you didn't exactly introduce me," he pointed out, sounding hurt.

I pulled the door shut and skittered down the hall, still trying to absorb the shock. Since when did Laurel wear garter belts and have sex in her office? Since when did she have sex at all?

"Eva, wait." I heard Laurel's heels clicking on the floor as she chased me down. "Don't go."

I stopped, but didn't turn around. No way could I handle the sight of her in a thong. "It's okay." I tried to sound casual. "I'll come back later."

"No, no, it's fine," she insisted, sounding equally casual. "What's up?"

"I honestly can't remember."

She came around to face me, wearing, to my unending relief, Gavin's hastily buttoned white shirt. "Look. You're probably wondering what's going on with me and Gavin—"

"No, I think I have a pretty good idea."

"I like to keep my personal life private, but I guess we got a little carried away when he came by to drop off his head shot."

"Head shot? He wants to be an actor?"

"Every waiter in this town wants to be an actor. Except for the ones that want to write screenplays." She smoothed her hair back. "And I'm, uh, helping him break into the industry."

I must have looked pretty shellshocked, because she reached out to squeeze my hand. "It's okay, pet. We've been seeing each other for a few weeks, but I didn't want to tell you until we were a little more—"

"Oh my God," I moaned. "I told you your boyfriend should be on the dessert menu."

She laughed. "Yes, well, obviously I agree."

"I'm going to die of embarrassment."

"If anyone's going to die of embarrassment, it'll be me," she corrected, tugging the shirt down over her thighs. She ushered me into an empty office and tried to look businesslike. "So what did you need to talk about?"

What *did* I need to talk about? My mind had gone completely blank.

"Eva," she prompted. "You showed up here for a reason, right? Is there a problem?"

Problem. Problem. Oh yeah. "It's Coelle," I stammered, looking everywhere but at her. "She got fired from *Twilight's Tempest*."

Laurel nodded. "I know."

Oh. I guess it would make sense that they would tell the agent. "And she passed out on-set last week. Twice."

Another nod. "I know."

"And Jacinda thinks she's making herself throw up again."

"That I didn't know. But I suspected." She leaned back against the desk, looking thoughtful. "Well, at least we'll catch it early this time. Thanks for telling me."

"So what are you going to do?"

"I already called her mother."

"No, no!" I protested. "Coelle's going to—"

"Pet." The cold, steely, no-nonsense Laurel was back. Wearing a lacy garter belt. *Aiiigh.* "Coelle is her *child.* She has to be informed."

"But—"

"She's flying out tomorrow. I'm going to pick her up at the airport at ten."

"But—"

"And you're coming to the airport with me." Laurel's smile was tight and forced. "We have a few things to discuss."

I shook my head. "No, we don't."

"Yes, we do." She bent over to straighten her stocking. "Pick you up at nine. And listen . . ." Her gaze drifted down the hall. "Keep this to yourself, would you?"

"Sure." I shrugged. "What's one more family secret?"

"Hi, Evie. Thanks for coming," Laurel said the next morning as I clambered into the sleek black Lincoln. "Not that you had a choice, but . . ."

"Listen, if this is about you and Gavin, I won't tell anyone. I swear," I said, a little too loudly. "And you know what? I'm fine with it. It's very trendy, very now, right? Very Ashton and Demi."

She waited for me to finish babbling, then got right back to her agenda. "I'm only going to ask you this once, and I want the truth." She leaned way into my personal space. I could smell the Altoids and coffee on her breath. "When Daphne Farnsworth gave you that check, did you sign anything?"

"Oh." I sank back in relief. "No."

Her lips thinned into a white line. "Are you sure?"

"Very sure. Between her and the creepy lockjaw butler, I

barely got a word in edgewise, forget about a signature."

"Fine. Okay." She sat back, relaxing. "I just want to make sure."

"Why? What's going on?"

She gazed out the window at the passing traffic. "I'm not sure yet, but have you gotten any unusual phone calls lately? Like, from lawyers?"

I shrugged. "Uh-uh."

"Good. Good."

"Should I *expect* to be getting phone calls from lawyers?"

"I don't know yet. I've heard a few . . . rumblings about your father. Nothing definite, just rumors. At first I thought that Daphne wrote you that check just to be a pompous witch, but now I don't know. I'm starting to think that maybe she had an ulterior motive."

"Like what? Could you be *any* more crytpic?"

"I don't mean to be vague, but I need to talk to your mother before I say anything else."

"Yeah, well, according to Gigi Geltin, she's brunching her way through the Valley with random middle-aged men. So much for her epic soul-searching quest." I snorted in disgust. "Ha. 'Fresh start,' my ass. More like fresh meat."

"Well, it's a good thing I didn't deposit that check yet," my aunt murmured, mostly to herself. "Just in case."

"In case *what?*" I pounded the seat in exasperation. "Come on. Just tell me."

"I can't. Not yet."

I exhaled loudly. "You drive me nuts."

"The feeling is entirely mutual, pet."

Mrs. Banerjee was waiting by the curb of LAX with a uniformed Skycap and a pile of Hermès luggage. Tall and slender, with glossy black hair halfway down her back, huge sunglasses, and an ankle-length mink coat, she looked like she'd come fresh from shopping on Fifth Avenue or skiing in Gstaad.

"Dude, how long is she staying?" I eyed the mountain of suitcases and garment bags. "Two years?"

"A few days, maybe. Now be nice."

I smiled sweetly. "I'm always nice."

"If only that were true." She straightened her collar as the car's chauffeur opened the back door. "Let's go."

"Felice. How are you? So nice to see you again!" Laurel stepped onto the curb and performed the requisite double air kiss, which Mrs. Banerjee returned with equal aplomb.

"Laurel, da*rrr*ling, *ciao*." Coelle had told me that her mother was born and raised in the States (New Jersey, to be exact), but she spoke as though she'd recently learned English in Milan. She peered into the car. "Where's Coelle? I fly all this way to see her and she won't even come to the airport?"

I waggled my fingers at her. "Hi, Mrs. Banerjee. I'm Eva. Coelle's roommate."

"My niece," Laurel explained. "We haven't told Coelle you're coming because, well . . ." She took Felice's arm and steered her out of my earshot. They bent their heads and murmured in low, urgent tones while I strained to eavesdrop.

"Poor thing," Felice was saying when they finally came up for air. "I've already called and made the arrangements. We leave for Oklahoma tonight. The most important thing is to get my little girl help. I knew I shouldn't have let her move back out here all by herself, but she was so insistent, and her father refused to let me leave New York . . ." She dug a Kleenex out of her handbag and dabbed at her eyes. "I've put too much pressure on her, haven't I? And she's punishing herself for my mistakes."

Coelle had always denounced her mother as a narcissistic, cosmetic surgery-obsessed, pretentious label whore, but the woman standing in front of me seemed genuinely concerned about her daughter.

"Let's not point fingers or place blame," Laurel said smoothly. "She's going to get the help she needs, and—"

"But imagine that she were your daughter, Laurel. Imagine that she were the most precious gift you'd ever been given and you let her move to Los Angeles alone when she was sixteen and then . . . well, *this* happened. Could you live with yourself?"

Laurel simply put an arm around her and helped her into the Town Car while the chauffeur crammed her luggage into the trunk.

Once seated, Felice blinked back her tears and smiled at me. "Eva, right?"

I nodded.

"Well, I'm delighted to finally meet you." She reached over and gave me a luxurious, minky hug. Her arms were strong and warm and she smelled faintly of lilies. "Thank you for being such a good friend to her."

I hugged her back, suddenly nostalgic for the Norman Rockwell childhood I'd never had. "Well, it wasn't me, really. Jacinda is the one who—"

"Thank heavens your aunt called me when she did." Felice shook her head. "Coelle hadn't even told me she was fired, can you imagine? Because she thinks I'm a horrible mother. Because she's afraid I'll be as hard on her as she is on herself. Well, that all stops today." Felice set her jaw resolutely. "I'm taking my baby to Oklahoma and we're not leaving until she's one hundred percent healthy. She deserves the very best."

"What's in Oklahoma?" I asked.

Felice obviously wanted to start crying again, but she held it together. "The best eating disorder clinic in the country. She can deny there's a problem till she's blue in the face, but she's going."

I nibbled my lower lip. "We tried to do, like, a mini-intervention before, but that didn't go so well."

"Telling Laurel was the right thing to do," Felice assured me. "Oh, that reminds me. I got you something. A little thank-you for watching over my daughter." She fished a box out of her bag.

A small, square, robin's egg blue box. With a white ribbon and the words "Tiffany & Co." stamped across the top.

I grinned up at her. "Any chance you'd consider adopting a sister for Coelle?"

"I already packed her a bag," Jacinda said by way of greeting when we knocked at the door. "She's ready when you are."

"Who is it?" Coelle called from the kitchen. "Is that Quent—" She broke off when she caught sight of her mother. "What are you doing here?" She recoiled as if she'd been shot. "And what are you wearing? Is that *real fur*?"

"Darling, be reasonable," Felice soothed, holding out her arms for a consolatory hug. "I've told you a thousand times, I inherited this coat when your grandmother died. I know how you feel about the fur industry, but this has been in the family for generations."

"Generations of *murder*," Coelle spat. "But I guess you put vanity ahead of the lives of poor, defenseless animals."

"Actually, minks are vicious little demons," Jacinda threw in. "Seriously. Vicious. You ever been to a mink farm?"

At that, Coelle stopped waging her one-woman war on fur and pointed an accusatory finger at Jacinda. "You guys called her, didn't you?" She spun around to jab her finger at me. "And picking her up at the airport? Why don't you just poison me with strychnine and then skin me while I'm still writhing on the ground?"

I blinked. "Don't you think that's a little harsh?"

"That's what happens to mink," she retorted. "Mom."

"Coelle, darling." Felice handed her offensive outergarment to my aunt and rested her hand on her daughter's shoulder. "Don't lash out at your friends. Laurel called me, if you must know. But they're worried about you, too. We all are."

"Oh, don't start with your perfect mother routine!" Coelle yelled. "You might fool them, but I know the truth."

Felice looked weary and jet-lagged. "You can hate me as much as you want, but you'll have to do it on the plane. Get your suitcase and let's go."

"I'm not going back to Oklahoma!"

"You have to, darling."

"There's nothing wrong with me!"

"This is not your decision, young lady. I am not asking, I am telling."

"Hell no, I won't go." Coelle raced up the stairs, into the bathroom, and slammed the door.

"Oh Lord." Felice looked to the rest of us for assistance. "I don't suppose any of you have keys?"

"Nope," I said.

"I used to be able to pick the lock, but she stuck bubble gum in there when she figured out I was on to her," Jacinda said. "Sorry."

Laurel stepped in to take charge. "We'll call a locksmith."

"No, no." Felice's face went pale. "I don't want a scene. The last thing we need are filthy rumors about this showing up in the tabloids."

"Then what, exactly, do you propose we do?" Laurel asked. "She could be in there for hours."

Felice dusted off her chic black dress and started toward the stairs. "You're a savvy businesswoman, Laurel. You know what we do next: we negotiate."

We trouped up behind Felice, who pounded on the bathroom door. "All right, if you want to play hardball, let's play. What's it going to take to get you out of this apartment and onto the plane to Oklahoma?"

Laurel, Jacinda, and I craned forward to hear the response, but there was only silence.

"I know you have your price, darling. What do you want? A Lexus? A new wardrobe? A weekend in St. Tropez with my credit card?"

"Go away!" Coelle shouted. "I hate all of you."

"I'm sure you do. But I know you have something in mind, so why don't you save us both time and just tell me what you want?"

"A diamond necklace?" Jacinda suggested.

I rolled my eyes. "Would you get off the diamond necklace already?"

"This could go on all afternoon," Laurel said. "I'm calling a locksmith."

"Did you hear that, Coelle?" Felice asked. "Laurel's calling a locksmith. So if I were you, I'd hurry up and bring an offer to the table!"

Long pause. Then: "I want my trust fund."

Felice looked like someone had just slipped *her* some strychnine. "What?"

"I want you and Dad to sign over all my earnings from the past seventeen years."

"You're not allowed to touch that money until you're twenty-five."

"I want it now."

"Why?"

"For college."

"Darling, you know Daddy and I will pay for college."

"Yeah, when I'm thirty-two and you've finished living vicariously through me."

Felice's hands fluttered to her collarbone. "Well, now you're just being hateful."

"You can fool my roommates, but you can't fool me. I want to apply to college this summer and I want you to promise to pay for it. Those are my terms. Take them or leave them."

"Well, that's . . . that's outrageous! You can't bully me. I'm going to let Laurel call the locksmith."

"Go ahead. Drag me out and stuff me in the car. I'll throw the biggest diva snit fit you ever saw at the airport."

"You wouldn't."

"I'll curse at the ticket agent. I'll joke about explosives when they screen my baggage. I'll . . . I'll *spit* on the flight attendant. And then, when it all ends up in the papers, I'll say I was high and I don't remember a thing."

"Whoa. *Now* we're playing hardball," Jacinda marveled.

"Coelle, this is just your anger talking."

"I apply to college when I get back from Oklahoma. Deal?"

Felice switched tactics. "But, honey, think of your career. Leaving *Twilight's Tempest* is actually a blessing in disguise. You can start doing movies! Wouldn't you rather be posing for photos at Cannes than stuck in some suffocating classroom?"

"My offer expires in ten seconds. Ten, nine, eight—"

"Fine. Go to college. If you're determined to throw away a lifetime of hard work, I can't stop you."

The lock gave way with a gentle *snick.*

"All right, then." Coelle brushed by me on her way to her bedroom. "Let's get this show on the road."

Fifteen minutes later, she was heaving a bulging black suitcase over the banister and into the living room. She refused to speak to either me or Jacinda as she hustled out the front door and into the waiting Town Car.

" 'Bye," I called weakly after her. "Call me when you get there, 'kay?"

"Yeah, we'll record *Animal Precinct* for you," Jacinda added.

She didn't even look at us as she climbed into the car.

"I'm so sorry." Felice sighed. "She'll get over it." Then the world's most perfect, elegant, empathetic mother turned to Laurel with a smile on her face. "And I'll try to make sure she's back in time for the Daytime Emmys."

Laurel blinked. "Oh, well, let's not worry about—"

"This is going to be her year," Felice said with feverish intensity. "I can *feel* it. And we'll use that to springboard her to a prime-time series and features."

"But . . . what about college?" I asked.

"Oh. That. Well, she's got psychological problems, Eva. She's not thinking clearly. She doesn't know what she wants right now."

"But you promised," I pointed out.

"We didn't put anything in writing, now did we? There's a little saying in this town: Verbal agreements aren't worth the paper they're printed on." She blew us a kiss, climbed into the Town Car, and sped off to Oklahoma with our roommate in her diabolical, mink-lined clutches.

So much for the dream mom routine.

"Holy shit," Jacinda breathed. "What have we done?"

20

I arrived at LAX at 4:30 A.M., my logic being that if Danny's flight left at seven, the earliest he'd get to the airport would be 5:00. I hadn't bothered going to bed; I'd spent most of the night worrying about Coelle, watching TV, and trying to conjure up the perfect words to say when I saw him. The words that would make him change his mind. The words that would make him feel like he used to.

Problem was, we had passed the point of words and moved on to a whole new plane of bitterness and chaos. So I had taken a lesson in man wrangling from Jacinda and dolled up in a tight, low-cut red dress, scarlet lipstick, and stripper heels. "It's harder for guys to be mad at you when all they want to do is rip your clothes off," she'd pointed out.

I set up camp on a row of cracked plastic chairs near the sliding doors and arranged my coat and bag on the seat next to me, ignoring the speculative looks I attracted from businessmen straggling off the red-eyes. "Keep walkin', buddy," I snapped. Then I plugged into my iPod, hoping that dance music at top volume would keep me alert.

Danny rolled in—*finally*—at 5:45, after four cups of lukewarm airport coffee had soured my stomach and my nervous anticipation had dulled into bleary-eyed angst. I was no longer feeling sexy in my tarty little outfit. Just slutty and ready for an Advil or five (note to self: never wear three-inch heels to a crack-of-dawn airport stakeout again).

He breezed right past me, looking rumpled but yummy in his usual jeans and baseball cap. Evidently, he'd skipped the shave this morning—he had a very sexy, stubbly look happening on his jawline. I leapt to my feet, grabbed my purse, and tapped his shoulder as he got in line to check his luggage at the automated kiosk.

"Danny!" I kept my tone flirty, as if we were meeting for cocktails. "Hi!"

"Eva?" He waited a few seconds before turning around, like he was hoping this was all a bad dream.

"Yeah, I . . ." Where were all the perfect words I'd spent all night composing? "I wanted to talk to you. Before you left for Florida."

"It's"—he checked his watch, still not turning around—"six in the morning."

"Five forty-five, actually. You're cutting it a little close, don't you think?"

"This is crazy. What do you think—" He finally risked a glance back over his shoulder, at which point he broke off midsentence. "You look good."

Score one for Jacinda. "Thanks. Listen, I know you weren't expecting me to show up like this, but—"

"Yeah." He jerked his gaze away from my (push-up bra-enhanced) cleavage and whipped back around. "Because I told you not to. I told you I didn't want to see you, or talk to you, or even think about you." We shuffled forward toward the check-in counter.

"I understand, but—"

"Then why are you here?" He pulled the brim of his base-ball cap lower on his forehead.

I reached out to touch the folds in the back of his sweat-shirt but chickened out before I made contact. "I wanted to see you. I couldn't let you go without—"

"You let me go when you started scamming on Jeff."

"I know," I said softly. "But I want to say I'm sorry. To your face."

"Okay, well, I hear you."

"And . . . ?"

"And what? What do you expect me to say?"

I stared down at the dirt-scuffed floor tiles. "I don't expect anything. But I know what it feels like to be lied to and disap-pointed. And I can't stand that I did that to you."

He focused all of his energy on printing out his boarding pass.

"You have every right to hate me."

He stiffened. "I don't *hate* you."

"Then what do you feel?"

A uniformed airline employee arrived at the kiosk to help him check his bag, which gave him the perfect opportunity to ignore my question.

"Danny? Hello?" I trailed after him as he threw his backpack onto his shoulder and headed toward the escalator.

"I'm going to Orlando," he announced when I caught up with him.

"I heard. That's why I'm here."

He kept walking. I kept following. We were starting to create something of a stir. My red dress wasn't exactly designed to blend into the scenery.

"You never answered my question," I reminded him as we stepped onto the escalators. "I asked how you felt about me."

"Don't ask me that right now."

I squeezed my eyes shut and said, "I meant what I said on the phone last time. I love you. I did when we, um, when we tried to, um, when we were at the Somerset Hotel. I should have said it back to you."

When he didn't say anything, I opened my eyes.

"I've never said that to anyone before," I told him. "You're the first guy I've—"

"Stop." His hand slammed down on the escalator safety rail. "Will you just stop?"

"I know this is all wrong." I gestured to the grim-faced

travelers bustling by us. "But I have to know if there's still a chance we could try to work stuff out. If there's even a teeny, tiny chance that you might still love me, too . . ."

"I can't."

"You can't or you don't?"

He shrugged.

"Oh no." I put my hand up. "Don't you shrug at me. I will not be shrugged at. You *can't* love me or you *don't* love me?"

A short, grumpy security agent on a power trip interrupted us with, "Boarding pass and ID, please."

"I'm going to Florida," he said stonily.

"I know that! So? What does that have to do with anything?"

"I can't decide everything right now. I have to make this flight. I have to think about pitching."

"Then don't think! Just feel!"

"Maybe I'll call you when I get back," he said. Clearly lying.

"So that's it? 'Don't call me; I'll call you'? Like I'm some nameless wannabe at an audition? Like the whole thing between us never happened?"

"Boarding pass and ID, sir." The security agent's Napoleon complex was raging out of control.

Danny handed over his driver's license and ticket, then looked at me. "We're going in different directions."

"Like Florida?" My desperate attempt at humor didn't elicit a smile from either of us. "But you're coming back, right?"

"I can't do this." He turned his back to me and took his

place in line, and this time he didn't look back. He placed his backpack on the conveyor belt and disappeared through the metal detectors.

And then I was all by myself at the back of the line, just another heartbroken girl in a too-bright dress waiting for a romantic Hollywood ending that was never going to happen.

21

The ride home from the airport was completely depressing, and the huge traffic jam on the freeway didn't do much to improve my mood. Neither did the fact that the Goose's crappy radio picked up exactly one station—the twenty-four-hour "fiesta mariachi" channel.

Why could I never recognize the best things in my life until I'd already thrown them away? Maybe I was permanently screwed-up from my childhood. Maybe I secretly thought I deserved to lose the people I loved.

Or maybe I was just a complete dumb-ass who should've

kept my pants on when Jeff showed up at my door in the middle of the night.

I parked the Goose a block away from our building and trudged toward the apartment, praying that Jacinda would still be asleep, because I couldn't talk to anyone right now. I just wanted to curl up in bed, pull the covers over my head, and cry until my exhaustion finally overcame my sorrow.

As I crossed the grassy courtyard, cold morning dew splashed my bare toes, and I hugged my coat tighter around me. Fifty feet to go until I could close the door on the world. Forty feet. Thirty.

I squinted as I neared our apartment, trying to discern the figure outlined by the blinding sunlight. Tall and thin and deliberately posed to show her best side.

We both froze, sizing each other up.

"Eva?"

"Mom?"

She must have seen something in my eyes, because her face crumpled and she opened her arms to me. I stepped into her embrace, wordlessly squeezing back. She didn't ask why I was traipsing home at 7:00 A.M. in crimson heels and a minidress. She just held on to me and, for the first time in fourteen years, I let her.

"I'm so angry at you," I muttered into her hair.

"Of course you are, baby girl."

And then, before the tears could start leaking out, I pulled back and looked behind her.

Another blurry figure waited by my front door. He came into focus as he walked toward us—rangy and broad-shouldered with an easy gait. I'd never seen him before in my life, yet he seemed familiar. Just when I convinced myself that yep, this time I'd finally lost the few remaining shreds of my mind, he smiled and extended his right hand.

"Hi," he said. "I hear you're looking for me. I'm Thomas."

As many as 1 in 3 Americans
have HIV and don't know it.

TAKE CONTROL.
KNOW YOUR STATUS.
GET TESTED.

To learn more about HIV testing,
or get a free guide to HIV and
other sexually transmitted diseases.

www.knowhivaids.org
1-866-344-KNOW